I0601888

CAPTIVATING THE HEART OF THE BILLIONAIRE

KNOX BROTHERS OF ARBOR SHORES BOOK TWO

NOMI SUMMERS

Copyright © 2019 by Nomi Summers

All rights reserved. No part of this publication may be reproduced, distributed, or transmitted in any form or by any means, including photocopying, recording, or other electronic or mechanical methods, without the prior written permission of the publisher, except in the case of brief quotations embodied in critical reviews and certain other noncommercial uses permitted by copyright law.

Write from the Heart Books
P.O. Box 66202
St. Pete Beach, FL 33736

Cover Design by Elizabeth Mackey Designs

ISBN-13: 978-1-7332773-3-4

This is a work of fiction. Names, characters, businesses, places, events, locales, and incidents are either the products of the author's imagination or used in a fictitious manner. Any resemblance to actual persons, living or dead, or actual events is purely coincidental.

CHAPTER 1

"Hey, bud, how was your day?" Rylee Benton asked her son as she walked into Arbor Shores Daycare. Liam was sitting at a table by himself, as usual. The few kids that were left waiting for their parents were gathered around playing together, but it was no surprise that she'd find Liam drawing at a table by himself. It wasn't that the other kids didn't like him, at least she hoped that wasn't the case, he'd just always been that kid that kept to himself. He was more into painting and drawing than playing with electronics like the others, and Rylee was grateful for it.

"It was awesome! We had a guest teacher come in today and show us painting with watercolors. Look, I'm making this for you." Liam looked up with bright eyes and handed over the art project he'd been working on.

Rylee took the painting from her son and held it up. It was a sunset lake scene with a blend of red, gold, and orange watercolors, which melded into three different shades of blue. This wasn't the work of a typical seven-year-old. Her son was clearly talented.

"That's us." Liam stood up so he could point out the two of them on the shore. "And that's Duke. We don't have him yet, but I just know someday you're gonna surprise me with him," he said, his eyes hopeful.

"Liam, we've been over this. Dogs are a lot of responsibility, and we aren't home enough right now to take care of one. Someday, bud. I promise." She ruffled his sandy blond hair and kneeled down to give him a squeeze, but inside, her heart plummeted. Looking at the painting was a painful reminder that it was just the two of them. She'd love more than anything to get him the puppy he'd always wanted, but she worked two jobs, so there wouldn't be anyone home to train the dog or give it proper attention. Liam's daycare was expensive, and she was thankful she at least had her parents to watch him in the evenings when she went to Ripples to wait tables.

"Ms. Benton, so nice to see you." Clarise, the daycare owner, came over and greeted her with a smile. "May I talk to you privately for a moment?"

"Of course." Rylee forced a half-smile. This didn't sound good. She followed Clarise to the corner of the room, out of earshot of Liam. "What is it? Has Liam done something wrong?"

"Oh, heavens, no. Liam is a dream," Clarise started, and Rylee let out a sigh of relief. "I just wanted to give this to you."

Rylee took the pamphlet from Clarise and glanced at the front cover: *Interhaven Arts Camp for the Gifted.*

"What's this?"

"It's a summer art program that's starting soon just a few towns over in Interhaven. The director came here today to teach a specialty class for the kids. She asked me to give this to you for Liam. She says he has a real talent with his art, and this is just the age where he should be developing his skills." She lowered her voice to a whisper. "By the way, out of all the kids, she only invited Liam to apply."

Rylee beamed at the thought of Liam being invited into an art program. She flipped the brochure open and scanned through all the classes and techniques they'd learn during the two-week period. It was perfect for Liam. But when she turned it over, her smile fell. The tuition was far beyond what she had in savings, even with two jobs. There was no way she would be able to afford it.

"Thank you, Clarise. I'll think about it." Rylee quickly stuffed the pamphlet into her purse and headed back over to her son. "Time to clean up and gather your things."

"Ms. Benton," Clarise followed her but waited until Liam got up to wash his hands before continuing. "The program doesn't begin for a couple of weeks. You could apply now, and a deposit would hold his spot. Final tuition isn't due until right before the program starts." She gave Rylee a knowing smile. It was no secret the tuition would be out of her reach. She'd struggled to pay for daycare a few times, and had to ask for an extension more than once on her payment. The daycare was always happy to oblige because they enjoyed having Liam, but she suspected an art program would not be as accommodating, especially one for gifted children. Something tugged at her stomach. There was no way she could come up with that kind of money. Shame flushed to her cheeks.

"Again, thank you, Clarise." Rylee plastered a smile on her face, but inside she was crushed for her son. She was just glad Liam didn't know anything about the program because he would surely want to attend.

She scooped up his backpack and filled it with his notebook and pencils, quick to grab her son's hand and head toward the door.

Rylee and Liam made their usual afternoon rounds. They stopped at home so Rylee could change work uniforms while Liam had a snack. From there, they headed to where her parents lived a town over in Belfort. Arbor Shores was a popular tourist destination and a place for the wealthy—a small coastal town west of Traverse City on the shores of Lake Michigan. Her parents had never been able to afford to live there, but they had managed to use her aunt's address when Rylee was growing up, so she could at least attend Arbor Shores school district, which was far better than the one she would've had to otherwise attend in Belfort.

Rylee had recently moved back to the area after being in New York City for the past eight years. She'd left Arbor Shores right after she graduated high school to study dance. She was accepted into the School of American Ballet on a scholarship, but life had different plans for her. She had returned home eight years later without her ballet slippers and with her seven-year-old son instead. A fair trade in her eyes. She loved her son more than anything, but it didn't mean she wasn't humiliated by some of her life choices or by the fact that she'd thrown away a full-ride scholarship to the best ballet school in the country.

She'd fallen quickly for her first love, Brandon Strauss, a hotshot stockbroker from Wall Street when they were introduced on a double date by a fellow ballerina she went to school with. From the start, she didn't fit into their high-class world and always felt she didn't belong in their social circle. In hindsight, she should have known it would never work. Against her better judgment, things got serious fast, and she and Brandon had eloped on a weekend getaway to Atlantic City. But their marriage was cut short when he walked out on her three months after they'd wed once she'd found out she was pregnant. He told her that a baby didn't fit into his lifestyle, and he'd demanded an annulment. She didn't contest.

Rylee was crushed, and she'd decided in that moment she'd raise Liam alone and never fall for a guy like Brandon again. She never saw a dime of child support from her ex because she didn't want him to have any rights to Liam, so she had chosen not to list him as the father on the birth certificate since their annulment was finalized before Liam was born. A decision that was best for all, especially since Brandon had never spoken to her again. He didn't even call when Liam was born, and she was sure he had heard the news through their mutual friends.

Being a single mother was not part of her plan when she'd moved to New York City, but she did what she had to do to give her son the best life possible. But that meant dropping out of school and working multiple jobs to make ends meet so she could raise him as a single parent.

When Liam began to get bullied at school, that's when she decided she needed to get him out of the inner city school system in New York and relocate back to Michigan. Now situated in Arbor Shores, she was happy to pay the high Arbor Shores rent so he could go to a good school, but that meant working two jobs and living paycheck to paycheck.

"How's my handsome grandson?" Mary Benton opened the door to allow Liam to enter, wiping her hands on her apron. The sweet scent of apple pie drifted through the air and met Rylee's nose in an instant.

"Hi, Nana." Liam stood on his tiptoes to give her a hug before moving past her to make his way into their home.

"Do you have time to come in for some tea? You look tired, Rylee."

"Not today. I want to make sure I have time to call Avery over at the resort. I'm going to see if she has any extra cleaning shifts for me."

"You're trying to pick up more work?" Her mother's brows pinched together. "What on earth for?"

"There is an art camp I'd like to send Liam to. It's far more than I can afford right now, so I just thought if I could pick up a few extra shifts—"

"And sleep when?" Her mother's voice filled with disapproval. "You've been burning the wick at both ends, and it's going to catch up with you. Mark my words."

"I'm fine, Mom. I can handle it." Rylee glanced at her watch. "It's a really good program, but please don't mention it to Liam. I don't want to get his hopes up in case I can't come up with the tuition."

"All right. Well, I sure wish your father and I could help you, but we just had to scrape up every last penny for a new roof. It took everything we had in our savings and then some."

"You know I wouldn't ask that of you."

"Well, you know we'd help if we could."

"I know you would. Thanks for keeping Liam. I should be back around ten to pick him up."

Rylee walked back toward her Toyota Corolla with her mother's words burning inside her mind. Did she really look that tired? Sure, she was a little fatigued, but nothing she couldn't handle. Her mother was one to talk. Rylee had learned her great work ethic from her parents, after all. Growing up, her parents never had two nickels to rub together, but somehow, they'd always managed to pay for her dance lessons. Her father, Paul, worked overtime in a local stamping plant, and her mother had taught school by day and worked as a clerk in the grocery store in the evenings just so Rylee could take all those classes. Now that Rylee was grown, her parents had slowed down, so they had even less than when she was growing up. She was just thankful they were more than happy to help with Liam, so she didn't have the added expense of a sitter.

Rylee backed her car out of the driveway of her childhood home and headed back down the winding evergreen-lined road toward Arbor Shores. She had a fifteen minute drive ahead of her, so she figured this was the perfect time to give Avery a call. Arbor Shores Resort was a large destination resort owned by the

Cooke family. Avery Cooke and Rylee had been best friends since they were young girls, and Avery was kind enough to offer Rylee a few shifts per week cleaning at the resort for extra income.

"Well, if it isn't my long lost BFF," Avery said into the receiver as she answered Rylee's call.

"Ha! I could say the same thing about you," Rylee teased back. Even though they both worked at the resort, she hadn't seen much of her friend lately. Ever since Shane Knox had come back to town, Avery had been spending every waking moment with him. How could she blame her? They had a once-in-a-lifetime kind of love.

"Yeah, I know. We've been really busy around here. Shane is helping me make the necessary changes to the resort to make it more eco-friendly."

"That's great. I know that's something you've wanted for a long time."

"So, what are you up to?"

"Actually, I was calling, not only to hear your lovely voice, but because I wanted to see if you had any extra cleaning shifts I could pick up at the resort? There's an art camp I'd really like to send Liam to, and I could use the extra cash."

"Oh, shoot. I wish I had known. I just hired a new person yesterday. She starts on Saturday."

Rylee's heart sank; she thought for sure she'd be able to get some extra shifts. She hadn't considered that Avery might hire someone. "That's okay. Thanks, anyway."

"Hey, I just remembered something. I overheard Shane's brother telling him that he's looking for someone to clean his house one or two days per week."

"Which Knox brother are you referring to? Please don't tell me Hunter." Rylee dreaded Avery's response, but there was only one answer she could give. Hunter was the only other Knox brother who lived in Arbor Shores.

"Yes, it's Hunter. But I'm sure he pays well, and that guy is seriously always working, so I doubt you'd even have to see him all that much."

Rylee paused to consider Avery's words. Was cleaning for Hunter an option she was willing to entertain? The four Knox brothers were legends in Arbor Shores, partly because of their striking good looks, and also because their father, Carter Knox, was one of the wealthiest men around.

"Actually, that would work because I only have time for one or two shifts somewhere. Will you find out the details and let me know?"

"Sure will. Shane is actually headed over to Hunter's house now. I'll try to catch him before he gets there."

"Thank you so much, Ave. I really appreciate it."

"Well, don't thank me just yet. Let me talk to Shane, and I'll call you back."

"My shift is starting at Ripples soon. You can just shoot me a text."

"Sounds good. Have fun at work!" The line went dead, and Rylee knew Avery would go to work on her behalf.

But could she handle working for Hunter? She didn't know much about him, except that he was on track to become the youngest billionaire ever to come out of Michigan, and she had a feeling that kind of wealth had probably gone to his head. Out of the four Knox brothers, he was the only one who stayed in Arbor Shores after high school to work in the family business. She'd overheard Shane telling Avery that after the recent heart attack of their father, Hunter was in the process of taking over Knox Enterprises so his father could finally retire.

She didn't know Hunter personally, but she suspected he was just like every other rich person: demanding and entitled. Just like Brandon. Still, if the job was available, shouldn't she take it?

It was a lot to consider, but she'd do anything for Liam.

CHAPTER 2

"*I*t's open," Hunter Knox called out to his brother who had just approached the front door.

"Hey, man. Nice pad," Shane said, entering his brother's lakeside home. He let out a long whistle as he turned in a circle to look around the massive estate.

Shane was the eldest of the four Knox brothers, and Hunter was the youngest. They hadn't had much of a relationship over the years, in part because Shane was a famous rock star and had just recently relocated back to Arbor Shores from California. They'd also grown up with four years between them, so they'd never really gotten close, and they couldn't be more opposite from each other. But their father's recent heart attack had brought the two brothers back together, and now they were working on forming the relationship they'd never had.

"Thanks, I bought it a year ago. I haven't done much with it yet, but the view of the lake is great, and I spend most of my time out back when I'm home, anyway."

"This place is stellar. Kinda big for just one person, though, don't you think?"

Hunter ignored the question, but the innocent remark from his brother still stung. He brushed it off. Shane didn't mean anything by it. But it was a painful reminder that he was, in fact, alone.

Hunter made his way across the open floor plan to the kitchen and grabbed two beers from the fridge. "Let's sit out back. You're gonna love the view."

The sliders that ran the length of the living room were already open, allowing the breeze from the lake to fill the home with freshwater air. The doors led out to a massive deck that reached all the way to the sand. Beyond the sand, a short trail between the beach grass opened to the shoreline of Lake Michigan, with blue water spread out before them for as far as one could see. Hunter had purchased a triple lot, so that he wouldn't have neighbors on either side. This gave him the privacy he cherished.

"Man, you weren't kidding. This place is right on the water."

Hunter twisted the cap off both beers and handed one to his brother before sinking into an Adirondack-style chair.

"How's Dad today?" Shane asked, taking a seat next to him. Shane and his father didn't have the best relationship, but Hunter suspected his brother would come around eventually.

"He's recovering. Slowly but surely." Hunter took a long pull from his beer and stared out at the water.

"Rumor has it you'll be taking over soon."

Hunter ran a hand through his sandy-blond hair. "Yeah, he's talking about retiring, although he hasn't officially announced anything yet."

"And then you'll become president of Knox Enterprises?"

"That's the plan."

"It suits you, bro. You always have loved the family business. I'm happy for you."

Hunter shot his brother a smile. Shane didn't seem to care that Hunter was set to become the sole heir of the family business. Shane had made it clear that he'd never wanted anything to do with Knox Enterprises. He was a famous rock star and lead singer in the band, Distant Union. Although he was taking a little break from the limelight, he'd made millions when the band was at their peak. Shane could never do another thing and still be set for life.

"I love what I do. Business is in my blood." Hunter held out his beer to clink it with his brother's.

"And music is in mine." Shane held out his own bottle.

Knox Enterprises owned commercial real estate all over the world, with their headquarters in Traverse City. From casinos to hotels to luxury condos to golf courses—they dabbled in just about everything. The Knox name was well known in the area, and Hunter was about to inherit it all.

"So, what did you want to talk to me about?" Shane asked.

Hunter cleared his throat and shifted in his chair to face his brother. "I'd like to throw you and Avery an engagement party here. I'm real happy for you two, and if it's okay with you, I'd like to put something together."

"Really?" Shane sounded surprised. "That's a kind gesture, but you don't have to do that."

"I know I don't, but I want to." Hunter hadn't even had anyone over since he'd bought the place, except for an occasional date here and there. This was the perfect opportunity to start building a relationship with Shane and break in his home at the same time. Plus, lately he'd been feeling like something was missing from his life. He realized he didn't have many friends anymore since all he did was work, and outside of work, he didn't have much of a social life. Sure, he had his acquaintances at the yacht club, where he had dinner most nights so that he didn't have to cook, but outside of that, he was pretty much a loner. A rich loner, with no reason to spend all the wealth he'd acquired.

"Well, we'd appreciate that. When were you thinking?"

"I thought maybe next weekend. That would give us a full week to get the word out."

"Will that give you enough time to prepare?"

"Yeah, it should. I'll have the food catered, and I'll bring in some entertainment."

"Music is my department. How about you let me handle that?" Shane laughed.

"Sounds good." Hunter grinned and took another pull off his beer. "I just really need to find a housekeeper before then. I want to get this place in top shape before the party."

"Your place is immaculate. But that reminds me, do you know Avery's friend, Rylee Benton?"

Hunter shook his head. "Doesn't ring a bell."

"Well, she cleans over at the resort, and she's looking for some extra work. She's a great girl; I think she'd be perfect."

"Is she trustworthy?" That was Hunter's number one concern. He was a private person, so letting a stranger into his home pushed him outside of his comfort zone. That's the reason why he had put off finding a housekeeper for so long to begin with. Plus, he was a bit of a neat freak and kept the place pretty spotless himself. But lately, he was working more than ever and didn't have time to keep up on it.

"Absolutely. Avery and I will vouch for her."

"All right. I'll give her a shot and see how she does. If it works out, I'll consider hiring her. When can she start?"

Rylee's last table at Ripples Bar and Grille wouldn't leave, and she got stuck working later than expected. Ripples was a waterfront attraction in the heart of Arbor Shores, always packed with tourists and locals alike, especially in the summer months. The tips were excellent on most days—weather permitting—and she had been lucky to land a waitressing job there.

When she finally made her way out to her car, she couldn't

wait to power up her cell phone to see if there was any word from Avery. To her delight, she had a text message:

You start tomorrow at 10 a.m. It's a trial run. The address is 137 Pine Ridge Way. Key is under the mat, alarm code is 8888. Hunter won't be there. If you do a good job, he's going to hire you. I know you will. Good luck!

She couldn't believe it. That was easier than expected, and tomorrow was perfect because she wasn't scheduled to clean at the resort on Fridays. Now she just had to do a nice job for Hunter. It was such a great opportunity; she couldn't afford to screw it up.

Elated, she turned on the radio and rolled down her window to feel the warm night air as she drove into the darkness toward Belfort to pick up Liam.

Liam might just get to go to art camp after all.

The next morning, Rylee awoke to Liam standing next to her bed.

"Momma, I don't feel so good."

"What's the matter, bud?" She sat up and placed the back of her hand across her son's forehead.

"My tummy hurts, and I feel tired."

"You have a fever. You can't go to daycare today, okay? You go lay back down and let me call Nana. I'll see if she can keep you while I go to work."

"Okay." She watched as her son shuffled back toward his bedroom. Rylee could tell he wasn't feeling well. It wasn't like him to miss daycare. He loved going there.

She took a quick shower, and got dressed in a red tank top and jean shorts. She brushed her teeth and threw her curly mane back in a ponytail. She was due at Hunter's in just over an hour, so she didn't have much time to find Liam a sitter. Hopefully her mom didn't have plans today.

"I'm so sorry, Rylee," her mom said into the receiver. "Your father's already at work, and I am running the Bake Sale at church today. You might just have to miss work this one time."

There was no way she could miss work today. This was her trial run. Who else might be able to watch Liam? She worked so much, she didn't stay in touch with many friends outside of Avery and Emma, and they both had businesses to run. There was no way she could ask either of them. She really needed to find a backup babysitter for times like these. Rylee dug at her temples. She had no choice; she would have to take him with her. Avery had said Hunter wouldn't be there anyway, so what was the harm? Liam was a good kid, he'd keep to himself and draw while she cleaned.

CHAPTER 3

*R*ylee headed south of town on Pine Ridge Way, a coastal road that ran parallel with Lake Michigan and lived up to its name. Towering evergreens on either side of the road hid the massive estates that sat back from the road. A surge of nervous anticipation swelled inside her. Rylee had never actually been inside one of the gigantic houses. She pulled right when she saw the mailbox in the shape of a lighthouse with 137 on the side in white numbers. Her jaw dropped as she traveled down the tree-lined driveway that opened to a lakefront mansion.

Rylee parked out front and helped Liam out of the back seat. She fetched the key from under the mat where Avery told her it would be. A heavy, wooden front door opened to a grand open-concept living area with pitched cathedral ceilings and white-washed wooden beams high above. The back wall of the house was all glass, allowing the light of the sun to brighten the home, and offering a clear view of Lake Michigan from every angle. Everything was light and airy. The kitchen had white cabinets with white marble counters. The rest of the house, from what she could see, was decorated in grays, blues and light wood, giving it a nautical feel. This guy had good taste. But how would she ever get through this entire place in one day? Surely it would take her all afternoon. Luckily, the home looked immaculate already. Not a hint of dirt anywhere.

"Momma, who lives here?" Liam asked with wide eyes. Rylee knew he'd never been inside a house of this size.

"You know Avery's fiancé, Shane? This is his brother's home."

"The rock star's brother lives here?" he asked, throwing his head back to look up at the ceiling. "This guy must be rich."

"Yes, he is," Rylee chuckled and began unpacking Liam's art supplies on the dining room table. "I want you to sit here and draw while I clean. Don't get into anything, okay?"

"I won't."

"I know you won't." She smiled warmly at her son and her heart broke for him. She hated to see him not feeling well.

"Momma, I'm thirsty."

Shoot. She had been running around trying to get him ready for the day and pack his art supplies, and somehow managed to forget to pack him anything to drink. Perhaps she could find him something in the fridge.

"Let me see if Mr. Knox has any juice." She opened the fridge and was shocked by its contents. Bottled Fiji water lined the top shelf next to a half gallon of milk and a few beers. Below that, a black takeout box, likely from somewhere fancy, sat on an otherwise empty shelf. The produce drawer held two red apples. How did this man survive without food? From the looks of his fridge, he was undoubtedly single.

She opened a water and found a glass in the cabinet, pouring half the bottle in and setting the glass in front of her son.

"I'm going to start cleaning upstairs. I'll check on you in a bit."

∾

Hunter took the curves on Pine Ridge Way at top speed in his Range Rover. He glanced at his Rolex. Quarter to one. He'd planned to make the trek home from the city around lunchtime but he'd gotten held up in a board meeting that lasted longer than expected. He wanted to stop in and meet Rylee before she was finished for the day. He couldn't shake the discomfort of having a stranger in his home while he wasn't there. What if she robbed him blind? Plus, there were certain ways he liked things done that he needed to explain to her.

He approached his front door and found it unlocked. His jaw clenched. He always kept his doors locked; even if Arbor Shores was a safe small town, you could never be too careful. One strike already. Stepping inside, he wasn't prepared for what he'd find next.

"Who are you?" A young boy sitting at his dining room table looked up and asked.

"I'm Hunter. May I ask who *you* are?" He made his way over to the kid to find a glass sitting on his custom-cut wood table, without a coaster. He grabbed one from the island and brought it over, picking up his glass and placing it on top of it.

"I'm Liam. Are you the guy who lives here?" he asked, putting down his pencil.

Hunter could just see it now, pencil marks on his table. He rubbed at the back of his neck as he studied the boy. "I am."

"My mom says you're rich."

"Where is your mother?" Hunter was growing impatient, although this kid was awfully cute.

"She's upstairs cleaning."

"Thank you. Nice to meet you, Liam."

"Nice to meet you," Liam responded before picking up his pencil and looking back at his drawing. Frustration grew inside Hunter. She should have put something down under his paper.

Making his way upstairs, Hunter could hear singing coming

from the bathroom of his master bedroom. He followed the sound until he found a woman on all fours, with her back to him, scrubbing his bathroom floor on hands and knees. Her dedication to detail was impressive, but why not just use the mop?

He watched and listened for a moment as she hit the high notes of "9 to 5" by Dolly Parton. She had a great voice, and her choice of song was quite humorous. Still, he couldn't shake the frustration that she'd brought her kid with her and they'd made themselves at home. In *his* home. This was not part of the deal. He made a mental note to have words with his brother.

Rylee had been cleaning for over two hours and had barely put a dent in the upstairs. How would she ever get the downstairs finished today?

Someone cleared his throat behind her, and it didn't sound like Liam. Startled, she whipped around quickly. "Oh, you scared me! I didn't expect you to be home so soon," Rylee said, rising to her feet and putting her sponge down to hold out her hand.

She'd recognized him as Hunter Knox, although she doubted he knew who she was. They had gone to high school together, but she'd been a few grades ahead of him. She'd seen him a few times at Ripples, but she'd never waited on him. He'd sat at the bar to eat the few times he'd been in. He looked down at her wet hand but did not return the gesture. "I'm Rylee," she said, dropping her hand next to her side and wiping it on her shorts.

"I didn't know it was bring-your-kid-to-work day, Rylee." His eyebrows shot up.

Warmth rushed to her cheeks. "I'm sorry, Mr. Knox. He normally goes to daycare but he wasn't feeling well this morning."

"Call me Hunter." He stood with his arms folded across his

neatly pressed suit. This man was well put together. He sure looked different up close with his chiseled jaw and striking blue eyes. A handsome man, no doubt, but not very warm.

"He's a good kid. I knew he'd keep to himself and draw. I hope you don't mind."

"Well, he's drawing on my dining room table without a coaster under his glass or anything under his paper."

"Oh, I'm so sorry. Let me go take care of that." She started to move past him, but he held up his hand, motioning for her to stop.

"That won't be necessary. What have you done so far today?"

"The upstairs. I was just getting ready to head downstairs to get started on the lower level."

"You mean you've been here since ten and you've only done the upstairs?"

Heat pricked at her skin, and she willed herself to take a breath. Rylee took pride in her work and was trying her best to do a nice job for him. Did he have any idea how large his home was?

A crash echoed through the house from downstairs. "Momma!" she heard Liam yell. This time, she pushed past Hunter and made her way down the winding staircase to find Liam's glass of water smashed on the floor. He stood in the middle of the mess, chards of glass all around him.

"Don't move, Liam." Rylee kneeled down and began picking up the glass. "What happened?" Her stomach was knotted with panic and humiliation. It was an accident, surely, but she didn't need this the first day on the job.

"I was getting up to go to the bathroom, and the glass slipped off the table." He turned to Hunter who had just made his way down the stairs behind her. "I'm sorry, mister."

"Don't touch the glass; you'll cut yourself," Hunter told them.

Rylee glanced over her shoulder to see Hunter approaching her with a broom and dustpan.

"I've got this. You can be finished for the day," he said. There was no denying the annoyance in his voice.

"But I'm not finished with the downstairs." She rose to her feet.

"If your son isn't feeling well, you should take him home." He held out the dustpan for her to drop the glass in. She could see his jaw pulse as he stared at her. She decided not to argue and to pack up Liam's backpack instead. But now, she was growing annoyed herself. Why was he being so cold? Clearly, it had been an accident.

"Come on, Liam. Go put your shoes on. Be careful of the glass." She guided her son toward the door and turned to face Hunter. "I'm really sorry about all of this. When would you like me to come back and finish?"

"I'll let you know," he said without looking up from the broom.

Had she really blown this opportunity on her first day? She grabbed Liam's hand and headed out the door, guiding him back to the car.

CHAPTER 4

*T*he weekend came and went, but Rylee never heard from Hunter. That must've meant she'd blown her shot for the cleaning gig, but she had filled out the application for Liam's art camp anyway, just in case.

On Monday morning, she awoke to an approval email from the director herself. Now it was real, and there was no way she could let the opportunity pass Liam by. She used what little was left in her savings to pay the deposit to hold his spot. She was more determined than ever to come up with the money for the rest of Liam's tuition, but how?

After she dropped Liam off at daycare, Rylee headed over to NovelTea Books & Tea House to meet Avery before her cleaning shift was set to begin at the resort. Avery had said she wanted to speak with her about something. Rylee was hoping she wasn't upset about what had happened at Hunter's. Avery did hook her up with the job after all, and had likely put in a good word for her.

NovelTea Books & Tea House sat on a wooded lot, down a side road, in the heart of Arbor Shores. Avery and Rylee's good friend, Emma, owned it, and it was one of Rylee's favorite places in town. She loved the smell of a bookstore, and she enjoyed a good book when time permitted—something her busy schedule hadn't allowed in quite some time.

She parked behind the building and followed the cobblestone path around to the front. Wildflowers grew sporadically along the front of the building, and stone benches were spread throughout the property as cozy reading nooks where customers could take their coffee or tea and find a private place to read. In the evenings, white twinkly lights illuminated the massive oak tree out front. Rylee made a mental note to try to get over to the shop more often. She always felt at peace there and loved the whimsical feel of the place.

"Morning, Em." She entered to find her friend on a ladder with her back to the door. Emma was writing the daily specials on a chalkboard behind the front counter. Today's special was Lavender Lemonade, and that sounded perfect.

"Rylee! It's so nice to see you here. What brings you in on a Monday morning?" Emma asked, retreating from the ladder and wiping her chalk-dusted hands on her apron.

"I'm meeting Avery. Is she here yet?"

"Here I am." The clunky bells on the door jangled as Avery entered behind them.

"Both of my girls are here! How exciting," Emma beamed. "What can I get for you two?"

"I'll try the Lavender Lemonade and one of those," Avery pointed out an oversized blueberry muffin inside the bakery case.

"Yum. I'll have the same," Rylee said.

"You two find a seat, and I'll bring it over."

It wasn't too hard to find an open seat since they were pretty much the only ones there besides one guy perched at the counter on his laptop, and an elderly lady perusing the romance section.

They chose a small table by the front window, and Emma delivered their order shortly thereafter.

It was clear to Rylee why Avery had asked to see her, so she would rather just break the ice and start with an apology. "Listen, Ave, I think I know why we're here," Rylee began, swiping at crumbs that had escaped her muffin and landed on the table. "I want to thank you for getting me the gig at Hunter's, and more importantly, I want to apologize for screwing it up."

"Screwing it up? Oh, no. What did you do?" Avery stopped mid-chew, a mouthful of muffin filling her cheeks.

"You mean, you didn't hear?"

"Hear what?" Avery resumed chewing slowly now, still wide-eyed as if awaiting her friend's story.

"When I woke up Friday morning, Liam was sick. I couldn't take him to daycare with a fever, and I couldn't find a sitter. I had no choice but to take him to Hunter's with me."

"Okay, but why didn't you just reschedule?" Avery asked.

"In hindsight, I wish I would have."

"So, what happened?"

"Well, Hunter came home, and let's just say he was not thrilled Liam was there. And then, Liam broke one of his water glasses on accident." She looked up at her friend.

"That's it? What's so wrong with that? I thought you were going to tell me there was some major catastrophe."

"Well, Hunter acted like it was a pretty big deal. He told me to leave and didn't allow me to finish cleaning. He hasn't asked me to come back." Rylee looked down and picked at a blueberry inside the muffin.

"I'll have Shane talk to him."

"No, please don't." She looked up quickly. "As much as I need the money, I don't think I can work for someone like him. He's pretty cold and wasn't the slightest bit accommodating. I'll figure something else out for Liam. I just want to put this thing with Hunter behind me. It was humiliating. I hope I never see him again."

"Well, that's going to be a problem." Avery had an amused grin on her face.

"Why is that?"

Avery fished a white envelope out of her purse and slid it across the table. 'Rylee Benton' was written on the front in gold calligraphy.

"What's this?"

"That's your invitation to Hunter's house this Saturday night. He's throwing an engagement party for Shane and me."

Rylee took that news like a blow to the gut. Just her luck. There was no way she could miss her best friend's engagement party. She plastered a fake smile on her face. "So that's why you asked me here?"

"Well, that's one reason. The other is to ask you if you'd be my maid of honor in our wedding?" Avery's smile lit up her face.

"Seriously? Of course! I mean, you know I'd love to be your maid of honor," Rylee beamed.

"We've decided on a winter wedding, and we want to do it this year. The resort is so beautiful at Christmastime. We can't resist."

"*This* Christmas? That's only five months away." Rylee nearly choked on the bite she'd just taken.

"Less than five, actually, but since my family owns the resort it's not like we have to find a venue, and we have all the vendor contacts already. I know we can pull it off. I want you to help me plan every detail."

Rylee got up and moved around the table to throw her arms around her friend. "Of course! I would be honored."

Emma appeared at the table, cupping a mug of tea. "What's going on over here? Did I miss something?" She blew on her tea before taking a sip.

"Perfect timing. I just asked Rylee to be in my wedding, and I wanted to ask you to be a bridesmaid. That's why I wanted to meet here this morning, so I could ask both of you."

Emma placed her mug on the table and motioned for Avery and Rylee to get up. Once on their feet, the three friends threw their arms around each other for a group hug. "Of course!" Emma agreed.

"This is going to be so much fun!" Rylee squealed. The man at the counter cleared his throat and the three girls regained their composure. Rylee and Avery returned to their seats.

"Don't mind him; he's always grumpy until his third cup of coffee," Emma whispered. "I'm so excited. You'll keep me posted on the details?"

"Of course. And here's your invitation to our engagement party this Saturday."

"I wouldn't miss it for the world." Emma smiled widely before retreating back to the front counter.

Rylee was filled with a mixture of excitement and nerves. Excited to be the maid of honor for her friend, and nervous that she'd have to see Hunter again. In his home, no less.

First things first, she'd need to get her Saturday night shift covered at Ripples, which meant she would be out even more money. But still, it was her best friend's engagement party, and there was no way she could miss it. Not for anything.

Hunter spent the morning working from home instead of going into the city. This way, he could order the catering for Saturday's engagement party, get the staff set, and finish cleaning the downstairs of his home, something he was now wishing he'd let Rylee do. He'd considered asking her to come back to finish the job, but then again, he didn't even have her phone number. Had he overreacted? No, he was sure she wasn't a good fit. Women with children were always having to call off or reschedule, and he needed someone he could count on—someone with more availability.

There was something about her, though, that he just couldn't get out of his mind. The way she sang when she cleaned had amused him, and the fact that she was scrubbing his floor on all fours instead of using a mop was impressive. Still, he'd decided that it wouldn't work, so he just needed to find someone else. But, who? In the meantime, he'd do it himself, something he wouldn't normally mind if he wasn't so busy at work.

He'd been putting in even more hours at work lately. Even though he was a shoo-in to take over Knox Enterprises when his father retired, he wanted to make sure Carter didn't have any second thoughts. Deep down, he knew his worries were unfounded. Who would his father put in charge if it wasn't Hunter, anyway? He was the only one of the four Knox brothers who ever wanted anything to do with the family business, and he'd worked his butt off over the past seven years learning everything there was to know about high-end commercial real estate. He'd excelled quickly in the company, and he'd become one of the youngest millionaires in the region. He was known for his tenacity in business deals, and he himself couldn't remember a time when he wanted something he didn't get. Hunter always rose to the top of every situation; all he hoped for was that his father had noticed his efforts. But one thing Carter never did was give praise. Sometimes it felt as though Hunter lived his entire life trying to earn something he would never actually have.

After a full day of cleaning, followed by a quick jog on the beach, Hunter decided he was getting hungry. Perhaps he'd head to Ripples to see Big John behind the bar and get some dinner. Hunter didn't cook much. Even if he'd wanted to, he never had food in his house. There was never any time to shop, which is another reason why he needed to find a housekeeper.

Most of the time, he ate in the city before heading back to

Arbor Shores in the evenings. Business dinners or takeout before leaving the office. When he did make it home early enough, he'd have dinner at the Arbor Shores Yacht Club where he was a member. But today, he was tired from cleaning and didn't feel like getting dressed up for the the club. He was famished, and he just wanted a hot shower and a good meal. Ripples was a place where he could go casual, and a burger was sounding mighty good at the moment.

He pulled his Range Rover into the Ripples parking lot. It was packed. Would he even be able to find a seat? It was summer, the time of year when their small coastal town flooded with tourists from downstate. Restaurants in town had a wait most nights, but it was a Monday. Hopefully, some of the tourists had headed out after the weekend.

To Hunter's dismay, every seat at the bar was taken. He headed to the hostess stand out on the back deck. It was a nice evening, so he'd sit outside if he could find a seat.

"Table for one," he told the hostess as he approached the stand.

"Let me see if I have anything. We're pretty full." She scanned the crowd of tables on the patio that backed up to the beach. The patio is where most people usually gathered, especially on a beautiful summer evening like this. The sun was starting to get low in the sky, and the sunsets over Lake Michigan were always spectacular, so it wasn't likely that anyone would be getting up until it had set. "You're in luck. I have one table in the corner. Follow me."

He followed the hostess as she zigzagged through tables and placed a menu in front of him on a two-top in the corner. "Your server will be right with you." She smiled and touched his arm before disappearing back to the stand. Was she coming on to him?

Hunter held up the menu and stared at it, unable to decide between the mega burger or the Walleye dinner.

"Hey there," the waitress said. "Can I get you something to drink?" He lowered his menu and his whole body stilled. Just his luck. Heat rushed to Hunter's cheeks; the look on the server's face told him she was just as uncomfortable to see him as he was her.

He was hoping he'd never have to see Rylee again after the way he had thrown her out of his home. He still felt bad about it, and now here she was taking his order. Didn't Shane say she worked at the resort? What was she doing at Ripples, anyway?

"I didn't know you worked here," he managed to get out with a forced smile.

The glow of the evening sun had cast a warmth on her face, accentuating her creamy complexion and pale blue eyes. She didn't wear much makeup; she didn't need it. She had a natural beauty about her that was refreshing, unlike the women he was used to. Her curly mane was pulled loosely back in a ponytail, with a few wild tendrils that had broken free framing her face. She was pretty, in a girl-next-door kind of way. How had he not noticed this at his house?

"Sorry. You're stuck with me," she said dryly as she leaned down to straighten the salt and pepper shakers on the table. It was obvious she was trying to avoid eye contact. "A drink, perhaps?"

"I'll just have water. Sparkling, if you have it."

"Sparkling?" This time she looked straight at him, head cocked, with a pitched brow. "No, sorry, we don't."

"An unsweetened iced tea will be fine. And I'm ready to order." He handed over his menu. She reached out to take it from him and their hands brushed, the feeling of her skin on his sending a tingling sensation straight up his arm. He pulled back and clasped his hands on the table in front of him. "I'll have the Walleye. Oil and vinegar for the salad. And I'll have vegetables instead of the potato."

"Anything else?" She shifted her weight.

"That will be all." He gave her the best smile he could muster up given his nerves, but it went unreturned. What was wrong with him? Nobody made him sweat in the business world, so why was this girl making him squirm? It was, in fact, business after all. She'd applied for a position, but she wasn't a good fit. He didn't have anything to feel bad about, did he?

Rylee turned on her heel and headed toward the waitress station. He watched her intently as she crossed the patio, smiling warmly at each guest that she passed on the way. He found it endearing that she took time to ask each of her co-workers if they needed anything before she headed back to her section. Shane had said she was a great girl; perhaps Hunter had been too hard on her and should give her another chance.

"Your iced tea, sir." She returned, placing the cup in front of him, barely stopping at the table to set it down before she was off to the table beside his.

Sir? She knew his name. It was clear, an apology was in order. If he could just get her to slow down long enough for him to have a conversation with her.

When she delivered his meal, he took that as the perfect opportunity to break the ice. "I wanted to talk to you about what happened the other day."

"Look, I'm busy here." She motioned to the tables around her.

"I know. I'll be quick." He sat up straight and cleared his throat, stalling to search for the right words. "I may have overreacted. You see, I was just shocked to find you'd brought your son without discussing it with me. I was annoyed by the glass breaking, but that doesn't justify my actions."

"It was an accident," Rylee said through pinched lips. "I'll reimburse you for your glass."

"No, don't be silly. It's not about that. In fact, I'd like to pay you for your time."

"There's no need. It was a trial run, remember? I didn't make the cut." She turned to head back toward the building. Man, she wasn't making this easy on him. How would he ever get her to forgive him?

~

Rylee couldn't wait to get Hunter out of her section. She was humiliated by the way he'd treated her at his home, and he was the last person she wanted to see.

"Lucky you," Jenny, a fellow co-worker, said as Rylee approached the computer.

"Huh?" Rylee asked.

"You have Hunter Knox in your section. He's only the most eligible bachelor in town, and not to mention, not too bad on the eyes."

Rylee glanced across the patio at Hunter. This casual look did make him a bit less intimidating than the suit he'd been wearing the other day, yet even though he was one of the best looking men she'd ever had in her section, she had no desire to go near him other than to finally deliver his check.

She printed his tab and put it in a black check presenter, placing it on the table in front of him before picking up his plate. She wasn't offering him dessert; she wanted him out of there as quickly as possible and dessert would only delay his leaving.

She watched from afar as he placed his credit card inside the check presenter and slid it to the edge of the table for her to pick up, which she promptly did. She ran the card, and returned the receipt to him.

"Have a nice evening," she said as she dropped it off, careful not to look him in the eye. She waited until he was out of the building before going back to the table to pick up the check. She stuffed the check presenter into the front pocket of her apron until the dinner rush had ended. When she finally pulled it out of her pocket, she could hardly believe her eyes.

He'd left her a one hundred dollar tip.

Furious, she slammed the presenter shut and shoved it back into her apron. Was this his idea of an apology? How dare he think he could buy her forgiveness with his money.

Hunter Knox was just a typical rich guy, taking the easy way out. Well, she would not be bought. If he thought that was going to make up for the way he'd treated her, he had another thing coming.

CHAPTER 5

*T*he rest of the week flew by, and Saturday came before Rylee was ready. She scrambled to find something to wear to the engagement party, but it had been some time since she'd gotten dressed up for anything, and cocktail dresses were not something she had on hand. She'd finally given in and called Emma to borrow something of hers. Since Emma was also single with no date for the party, the two had decided they'd get ready at Emma's house and drive to the party together.

After Rylee dropped Liam off at her parents' house, she headed to Emma's. She pulled her car in front of the large white Victorian off Main Street, and was thankful the roadside spot in front of the house wasn't taken. Rylee often wondered how her friend could handle living right in town with all the summer traffic, but Emma liked to be within walking distance of her bookstore; plus, the energy of the small downtown area seemed to suit her.

"How about this one?" Emma asked, holding up an elegant, midnight-blue satin dress, its long hemline brushing the floor while delicate spaghetti straps were the only thing securing the garment on the hanger. "It will look great with your eyes."

Rylee let out a long breath and crinkled her nose. "I don't know, Em. It looks kinda … formfitting." Despite her hesitation, she took the dress from her friend and headed to the bathroom to try it on.

Once she managed to slip into it and get the back zipper up, she walked out slowly and looked in the full-length mirror on the back of Emma's closet door. Her friend was right. It did bring out the blue in her eyes, but it also made the rest of her assets pop as well, and she wasn't used to wearing something so tight on her curves.

"Wow! You look fantastic!" Emma let out a low whistle.

"Is it too much? Don't you have anything that's a little, I don't know, looser?" she asked.

"Nope, this is the dress. It looks killer on you. You have to trust me."

Rylee gave herself another once over in the mirror and ran her hand over her stomach to feel the material clinging to her body. Elegant as it was, she didn't like feeling so exposed. She was usually much more conservative. Yet something about it *did* make her feel confident, and she had the figure to pull it off. She'd kept her dancer's body, even though it had been years since she'd studied ballet.

"Do you have the address to the party? I can't seem to find what I did with my invitation," Emma said, leaning close to the mirror to line her perfectly pouty lips.

"The party is at Hunter Knox's house. I know how to get there."

Emma stopped what she was doing and looked at her friend through the reflection in the mirror. "And you know where Hunter lives … why?"

"Don't ask. It's a long story. But I was there last weekend, so I can get us there tonight. I'll drive."

"Wait, you were there last weekend? At Hunter Knox's

house? Did you two go on a date? I want details." Emma turned to face Rylee with a hand on her hip. Her eyes lit up in excitement.

"Ha! I would never date someone like Hunter." Rylee's brow furrowed. "Shane and Avery hooked me up with a cleaning gig at his house. Except I blew it. Again, it's a long story."

"Well, make a long story short and give me the CliffsNotes," Emma said and turned back to the mirror to finish applying her makeup.

"I had to take Liam with me at the last minute. He was sick, and apparently Hunter doesn't like kids or something. He came home early, basically told me to leave, and didn't ask me back to finish." It wasn't the whole story, but that was the gist of it.

"Really? What a jerk." Emma made a look of disgust in the mirror. "I mean, he's a hot jerk, but a jerk no less." She giggled.

"You can say that again. About the jerk part. The jury's still out on the hot part."

"Well, I can promise you one thing," Emma said, turning to eye Rylee again.

"What's that?"

"That's one decision he's going to regret the moment he sees you in that dress."

"I doubt that." Rylee shook her head. "Hunter Knox wouldn't look twice at someone he'd hire to be his maid."

Emma smiled. "We'll see."

It was ten minutes to seven, and guests were beginning to arrive. Shane and Avery were already out back on the veranda, chatting with a few early comers, and Hunter had just made his rounds to ensure the food was on point and the catering staff had everything they needed. He wanted this party to be perfect, and so far, it was looking like he'd managed to pull this off with just one week to prepare. Thank goodness Shane and Avery had taken over the guest list and invitations. He wouldn't have known who all they wanted to invite, plus, he had enough to handle to get the rest of the party planned.

Hunter heard the front door open, and he turned to see who had arrived. All the air was sucked from his lungs when he saw Rylee standing there next to another woman he didn't recognize. He hardly spared the stranger a glance before his eyes were drawn back to Rylee. She looked different. Beautiful, but different. Her long curls were free tonight, not pulled back in a ponytail like the last two times he'd seen her. And that dress. She looked stunning in that dress. He couldn't take his eyes off of her.

Their eyes locked for a moment, but she quickly looked away when a member of the serving staff approached her with a tray of champagne, which she declined. What was she doing here anyway? It made sense since it was Shane and Avery that had recommended her for the cleaning position. But why hadn't he thought of that this week? With all that was going on, he'd never thought to consider that she'd be coming to the party.

He tugged at the bowtie on his neck, suddenly feeling hot in his tux. The party was a black tie affair, but now, he was regretting that decision. He took off his tuxedo jacket and handed it to the server that had just approached him with champagne. He took a glass and headed straight for Rylee and her friend.

"Good evening, Rylee. I didn't know you'd be coming," he said with a genuine smile as he approached them.

"Why wouldn't I be here?" she asked with half a laugh. "I'm the maid of honor."

"I didn't know that, either." Stunned at the news, he turned to Emma and held out his hand. "I'm Hunter Knox. And you are?"

"Emma Woods."

"Welcome, Emma. Thank you both for coming. Please, make yourselves at home."

They both nodded and moved past him to head toward the back veranda. He watched as Rylee glided across the room, smiling and saying hello to each member of the serving staff as she made her way outside.

There was just something about this woman that he couldn't put his finger on. She had a kindness that she shared with everyone she encountered. Well, everyone except *him*. Still, she wasn't like the women he met at the yacht club or some of the money-hungry ones he frequently found himself on dates with. Women typically flocked to him, but he never knew if they genuinely liked *him,* or if they were only attracted to his wealth and success. Because of that, he hadn't let anyone get close. He was guarded. But Rylee didn't seem impressed by him or his money, and that was both intriguing and a blow to his ego at the same time.

Why hadn't he seen her around in a town as small as Arbor Shores? He knew nothing about her, and he was beginning to realize he wanted to learn more.

If Hunter didn't know better, he'd think Rylee had spent most of the evening trying to avoid him. The party was winding down now, and the handful of guests that still remained had moved inside. He'd watched Rylee take her cell phone out back to make a phone call, and he took that as his opportunity to try to talk to her and make things right. He waited quietly while she finished her call.

"I won't be much longer, Dad. Tell Mom I'll be there to get Liam in about thirty minutes. Love you," she said before hanging up.

She had her back to him and was staring out over the water. He shoved his hands into his pockets and took his place next to her. "Nice night, isn't it?" he asked.

She glanced over at him. "It is," she agreed, putting her cell phone into her clutch and placing it on the railing of the deck.

Silence fell between them as he struggled to find the right words. All that could be heard was the subtle sound of the waves lapping at the shore. The beach grass rustled in the breeze, and with only the sliver of a new moon, it was a dark night. The sky lit up with what looked like a billion stars above.

"I'm glad you came," he finally said, looking out toward the water with her.

"Me too, because I want to ask you something."

What could she want to ask him? Was she going to ask for a second chance, because he wasn't prepared to make a decision about that just yet. Not with this attraction for her that was growing inside him. "Anything," he managed to get out.

She turned to face him. "Why did you leave me that tip at Ripples? Did you think you could just buy an apology? Because I don't work like that." Her face was serious, and he detected a hint of hurt in her voice.

"No, not at all." He turned toward her, shock jolting through his system. That wasn't what he'd expected her to ask. "I wanted to reimburse you for your time. It only seemed fair. You did a nice job here, and it was my way of saying thank you. And yes, I suppose, also as a way to say that I'm sorry."

"Well, I told you it wasn't necessary. We had a deal. It was just a trial."

"May I ask you a personal question?" he asked, changing the subject.

"That depends on the question."

She was guarded, and he could appreciate that. He'd have to tread lightly with her, but he wanted to get to know her better.

"Why did you want to work for me in the first place? I mean, you have two other jobs." His question was met with silence. "Is Liam's father in the picture?"

She hesitated for a moment longer, and he was sure that he may have overstepped his boundaries. "No, Liam's father is not in the picture," she finally said, turning back toward the water.

That twisted at his stomach. He couldn't imagine the thought of a boy growing up without a father. Sure, his own dad wasn't exactly father of the year. But as hard as Carter was on the Knox boys, at least they'd had a father. His heart hurt for Rylee's son. He shouldn't have kicked them out of his home.

"I'm just a single mother trying to give my son a good life. I was going to use the extra money for an art camp I'd like to send Liam to. That's all."

A lump formed in Hunter's throat. The more he spoke to Rylee, the worse his conscious gnawed at him. He couldn't help but think there was more to this woman. He was oddly intrigued by her, and he couldn't hold back his questions.

"And what about you?"

"What about me?" She shot him a puzzled look.

"What do you want for *you*?"

She looked taken aback by the question. "That's kind of personal, don't you think?"

"Forgive me if it is, and you don't have to answer if you don't want to. I'm just trying to get to know you better."

She hesitated, and silence filled the air between them once again. "Someday, I'd love to open a dance studio and offer ballet classes to children."

"You're a dancer?"

"Was. I moved to New York after high school to study ballet and start my career. I've been dancing my whole life."

"What happened?"

Rylee took a deep breath and let out a sigh. "A bad relationship happened. Then Liam came along, and I'm so thankful for that." She rubbed at her crossed arms. "I don't know why I'm telling you any of this."

Hunter looked at her in awe. "Listen, I want you to know I'm truly sorry for the way I acted. If you could somehow find it in you to forgive me, I'd love to have you come back."

"You mean you're giving me another trial?" She turned to face him with a look of hope in her eyes. Or was that desperation? Either way, Hunter knew she was the person for the job.

"No, not a trial. I'm giving you the job. If you still want it, that is." He gave her his most genuine smile and held his breath while he struggled to read her. "I mean, look at this place. I'm going to need some help cleaning up from this party for starters," he joked, hoping to lift the tension still lingering between them.

"I'm not working at the resort tomorrow. I could be here in the morning to get started. If you're sure?"

"That'd be great. Be here at nine." He smiled warmly. "Come on, let's head back inside. It's getting chilly out here."

Offering Rylee the job was a decision his mouth had made before his brain had a chance to analyze it, which wasn't the way he usually conducted business. Perhaps he felt bad for her, or maybe he felt bad for her son, but more than anything, he just wanted to spend more time with her.

He was ready to get to know Rylee better, even though the logical side of his brain was telling him it wasn't a good idea.

CHAPTER 6

*R*ylee dropped Liam off at daycare and arrived at Hunter's right on time. She pulled into his massive beachfront estate and a wave of relief washed over her. Landing this job was exactly the break she needed to pay for Liam's camp, and the final tuition payment was due at the end of the following week. They hadn't discussed pay yet, but she was hopeful that her first two weeks of cleaning salary would be enough to cover it.

"Good morning," Hunter greeted her with a smile as he opened the front door. He looked sharp in his three-piece suit. *He must be headed somewhere important.* For a moment, a pang of disappointment stabbed at her. Why did she think he'd be helping her? And why did she want him there, anyway?

"Morning." She returned the smile, making her way inside.

"Listen, I'd love to stick around, but my father called an impromptu Sunday meeting this morning, so I need to get into the city. I'm sorry to leave you with such a mess. The caterers cleaned up a bit, but I'm afraid there's still much to be done."

"It's no problem. That's what I'm here for."

"I have special cleaning supplies I'd like you to use on the marble. They're in the pantry across from the kitchen. Oh, and don't bother with my office. I usually do that myself."

Something about that didn't sit right with her. Did he not trust her? She chose to ignore it. She was determined not to blow this opportunity again.

Hunter pulled his wallet out of his pocket and handed her his card. "Here's my number if you need to get in touch with me." He moved toward the door. "And Rylee," He turned around to add with a wink, "I'm glad to have you back."

Me, too. But he was gone before she could respond.

Hunter arrived at Knox Enterprises ready for the big announcement. Energy surged through his system as he took the stairs two at a time, skipping the elevator completely. Fitness was an important part of his life; he was convinced it kept his mind sharp, and he attributed it largely as one of the keys to his success.

He was sure that his father had called this meeting to announce his retirement, which meant Hunter would be taking over as President of Knox Enterprises, something he had been working toward since he was eighteen. He'd always known it was coming, but he'd never dreamt it would happen this soon in his career. He was happy to take the responsibility of leadership off of his father so that Carter could enjoy his retirement. His father's heart attack had slowed him down, and he was getting to the age where it was time to travel and enjoy the wealth he'd worked his whole life to acquire. As far back as Hunter could remember, his father had been a workaholic and was always committed to the business. Growing up, his father had always put work before family, which meant he was seldom around for the important things a father should do with his sons.

As soon as Hunter graduated high school, he went straight

into the family business, working part time while he lived at home and attended Northern University. Once he'd graduated from college with his business degree, he'd gone to work for the company full time and had acquired his first million his first year out of college. He'd multiplied that first million every year since.

He was the only one of the four Knox brothers who wanted anything to do with the family business. The other three had left Arbor Shores as soon as they were old enough to make that decision. After Shane fled to California to pursue his music career and went on to become a famous rock star, his twin brothers both took off as well, just in opposite directions from each other. Ethan played college football for the University of Michigan before he went pro in the NFL. Chase, the other twin, was the wild card of the four Knox brothers. Nobody knew exactly where Chase was, but rumor had it he was somewhere in New York City. As a drifter, Chase did his fair share of traveling around, and Hunter had given up on trying to keep up with him long ago.

"Good morning, Mr. Knox," Maggie, the company's receptionist, greeted him from behind the front desk. "They're in the boardroom, ready for you."

They? Hunter assumed it would only be himself and his father in the office and at this meeting. Who else was there, and why?

"Thanks, Maggie," he managed to get out as he paused in front of her desk to catch his breath. He adjusted the jacket of his suit and buttoned it before heading to the boardroom.

Inside the boardroom, Hunter found his father sitting at the head of the table. To his right sat Marcus Bradley, a senior executive that had been with Knox Enterprises as long as Hunter could remember. In fact, he had been Carter's right-hand man until Hunter had shifted to full-time work in the business. Hunter had never quite cared for Marcus. There was something about him that made Hunter feel small. He'd always suspected Marcus was intimidated by his youth. Or maybe it was the fact that he'd slid into his position so quickly. When Hunter had started in the business, young and inexperienced, Marcus wasn't welcoming to him and didn't make anything easy on him. In fact, Hunter often wondered if Marcus went out of his way to set him up for failure.

"Take a seat," his father demanded, his tone firm. Neither of the men rose to greet Hunter as he entered the room. He took the seat across from Marcus who hadn't even bothered to acknowledge him.

"I've called you gentlemen here to make an announcement." Carter leaned back in his leather chair and pressed his fingertips together as he took turns looking between the two men. "As you probably suspect, the time has come for me to retire."

It was all unfolding exactly as Hunter had expected. He remained silent and waited for his father to continue, trying hard to stifle his smile.

"And as you know, one of you will be taking over as president of Knox Enterprises."

Confusion rippled through Hunter. What did his father mean by 'one of you'? Clearly, he was the logical choice for taking over the family business. He was a Knox, after all. Not Marcus. Plus, Hunter was already vice president of the company.

"I don't understand." Hunter sat up in his chair, anger getting the best of him. "Why would Marcus be considered for taking over the Knox family business? He's not family."

"Because Marcus has something you don't have, Hunter." Carter's words were sharp, in a tone that told him his father didn't appreciate being challenged. Hunter kept his mouth shut and let Carter continue. "Marcus has experience."

"I've been with this company longer than you've been alive," Marcus added in Hunter's direction. A snide smirk spread across his face as he leaned back confidently in his chair.

Under the table, Hunter's fists balled at his sides. "And again, no offense," Hunter said in Marcus' direction, "but Marcus isn't getting any younger. I bring something that Marcus doesn't have, and I feel that I've more than proven myself to this company over the past seven years."

Hunter could feel Marcus' eyes boring a hole into him now, but he couldn't take his eyes off of his father.

"Here's the thing." Carter sat up straight and set clasped hands on the table. "The decision is not only up to me. The board of directors is worried you might be too … immature, for lack of a better word, to handle the pressure and responsibility that'll come with the position."

"Immature?" Fire pulsated through Hunter. Sure, he might only be twenty-five years old, but he had busted his butt for his father's company and had proven himself time and time again. It's not like he was a party animal. Even in his college years, he wasn't out partying with friends. He was always one hundred percent committed to Knox Enterprises. How could his father do this to him?

"Marcus is a family man," Carter continued. "He has a wife and kids. Let's just say, he's settled. The board knows he's not going anywhere. You, on the other hand, are single, and you have your whole life ahead of you. It makes the board a bit nervous."

Seriously? He couldn't be in charge because he didn't have a wife or a girlfriend? It wasn't as if his father had let his family have any influence on how he ran the business when he was first starting out. Why did he care so much now? Hunter eyed Marcus dubiously. This sounded like his idea, his influence. "I'm not single," he spat out in a moment of panic. "I'm seeing someone, and I'm thinking about asking her to marry me."

"Oh? Why haven't I met her or heard anything about her?" Carter raised a brow at his son.

"It all happened so fast. We fell in love quickly, and I haven't introduced her to the family yet. She was at the engagement party last night, but I just didn't feel that was the right time. I wanted it to be all about Shane and Avery."

"Yeah, right," Marcus added under his breath from across the table.

"Excuse me? What do you know about my life, Marcus?" Hunter rose to his feet, jaw clenched.

"Gentlemen, that's enough." Carter raised his voice and Hunter sank back down into his chair. There was something about his father's temper that could shrink him in an instant, even as a grown man.

"Marcus, please excuse us. I'd like to speak with my son alone. I'll meet with you after," Carter said. Marcus shot Hunter a sly grin as he gathered his briefcase and headed for the door.

"So, who is this woman you're seeing?" Carter asked once the boardroom door shut.

Hunter's heart skipped a beat. He had to think fast. "Her name is Rylee Benton."

"Benton. I don't recognize the name. Is her family from Arbor Shores?"

Hunter realized he didn't know the answer to that question. "Yes."

"Well, bring her by the house for dinner this week. I want to meet her."

"Yes, sir."

"We'll be making a decision one month from today. That gives you four weeks to show the board you're ready to take over this company. I recommend bringing your girlfriend to the gala this weekend, as well, so the board can meet her." He tapped his pen on the desk before adding, "And I'd put a ring on her finger before you do."

Hunter just nodded in agreement. What had he done now?

"You know I'd love to see this company run by my son, but I have to do what's best for the business, and you have to convince the board you're ready. If you can show them you're ready to settle down and start a family, you'll have a better shot, and you'll have me in your corner. Or else, Marcus may be deemed a better fit."

"You know I can do this, Dad."

"It's not just me you have to convince."

"Consider it done."

Hunter sped back to Arbor Shores, taking the winding country roads between the city and the coastal town at top speed. He used the twenty-five minute drive to devise a plan. A plan that he had to make work, at any cost. His future was on the line, after all.

He opened the front door to his home and stopped to listen. He could hear singing coming from the kitchen. The sound luring a smile to his face.

"Hey there," he said, walking into the kitchen.

"Oh! You startled me." Rylee put down the sponge she'd been using inside the oven and rose to her feet. "I didn't expect you back so soon."

"This is becoming a common occurrence with us." He smiled warmly at her. "You have a beautiful voice," he added, and he meant it.

"Thank you." Her cheeks reddened as she looked down at her hands.

"I'd like to take you to lunch."

"Oh, that's not necessary. But, thank you." She turned and picked the sponge back up.

"Actually, I'd really like to talk to you about something."

"Am I fired again?" she asked over her shoulder. Her lips hinted at a smile, but he still couldn't tell if she was serious or making a joke.

"No, not even close," he tried again. "Have lunch with me?"

"I'm a mess. I can't go anywhere like this."

"You look fine." Aside from the black smudge of oven grease on her face, she really did look great. Even in her work clothes, with her hair piled high on top of her head, there was something refreshing about her. She'd looked stunning at the party the night before, but even now, something about this side of her looked just as beautiful.

She hesitated, and he waited with bated breath. What would he do if she said no?

"I have to be at Ripples for my shift in a few hours, and I still have a lot to do here. I'm going to have to pass this time."

He had to think fast. He hadn't considered a plan B. "Take a walk with me, then? It's a nice day for a walk on the beach, and I really do have something important to talk to you about. Please?" he added with his best smile.

"Okay," she finally said, and moved to the sink to wash her hands.

He studied her intently, pleased with his plan. He was sure she was the only person he wanted to pretend with for the next month. Now, he just had to convince her to say yes to his crazy scheme.

Rylee dried her hands and met Hunter by the glass doors that led out to the veranda. He slid it open for her, and as she made her way past him, he gently placed his hand on the small of her back to guide her. It was a subtle gesture, but one that shot an electric current right up her back. He led her down the path, through the beach grass, and to the open shoreline. The lake's cobalt blue water glistened in the sun before them. Hunter was right, it was a beautiful day. High seventies—not too hot—and the breeze from the lake was welcoming after the sweat she had worked up from cleaning.

Rylee couldn't remember the last time she had taken time to walk on the beach. She kicked off her shoes and dug her toes into the cool, wet sand. She looked down at Hunter's shoes. "Are you going to take those off?"

A puzzled look on his face, he gave her an amused grin and followed suit, taking off his shoes and rolling his dress pants up mid-calf. He was still in his suit, but he'd lost the jacket and untucked his shirt. Without the tie and with the top two buttons undone, he finally looked comfortable. She watched as he neatly placed their shoes up by the beach grass. He had a striking tan for someone who worked all the time, and she could tell his body was cut underneath his clothing. She wondered what he did for exercise. Whatever it was, it was working.

They began making their way down the shore, side by side. "So, what did you want to talk to me about?" she asked after they'd been walking for a minute or so.

"Rylee, I have a business proposition for you." He stopped and turned to her.

What kind of business deal could Hunter Knox possibly have for her? "Go on."

She stopped and looked up at him. His hazel eyes sparkled in the sun. She'd never quite seen them in this light, and they were mesmerizing. His features were striking, but she refused to look at him in that way. He was her boss now. Plus, she'd sworn off rich men after Brandon. Hunter had many of the same characteristics, which was a turnoff, even if he did look straight out of *GQ Magazine.*

"I don't know exactly how to put this, so I'm just going to come out with it."

"Okay."

"I need a fiancée. Just for a month. Well, two would be better, so it's more believable."

"What?" she snorted. *He must be kidding.*

"I'm serious. I'd like to hire you—no, I would like to propose a business deal to you."

She pinched her brows together. Did he just suggest hiring her to be his fiancée? He better hope for his sake she'd heard him wrong. She remained silent as she waited for him to continue, but with each second that passed, her blood pressure began to rise.

"This could be a win-win for both of us. You'll get the money for your son's art camp and—"

"Hunter, I hope you are not proposing that you pay me to be your fiancée. I've told you before, and I'll tell you again, I cannot be bought. I don't work like that."

A mixture of anger and hurt marinated inside of her. She was appalled by his audacity, and suddenly he wasn't as handsome as he'd been a few minutes ago. What kind of person tries to buy someone? *A Knox.*

"Please, hear me out." He took her by the hands and held them. She looked down at them, surprised by the gesture. "My father announced his retirement today, and the company might not go to me after all. The board is concerned that I'm a risk. I need to show them that I've settled down and that I'm ready to get married and become a family man. I need to show them stability, and you—"

"And you thought because I have a kid that you could just use Liam and me to create your instant family?" She pulled her hands away from his and placed them on her hips.

"No!" He scrubbed at his face. "It's not like that. I would never use you. I want to pay you for your time. It's a business deal, that's all."

"A business deal?" Her temper was threatening to get away from her. What kind of deal was this? If this was how the Knox men did business, then she wanted nothing to do with the entire family.

"Hear me out." Hunter pushed his hands through his hair and paused, as if to weigh his words. "I'll pay you fifty grand. You'll be able to send your son to camp, but you'll also be able to open your dance studio."

"I can't believe I opened up to you last night. You weren't trying to get to know me, you were fishing for information so you could come up with this plan." Humiliation added to the mix of emotions brewing inside of her. Why had she told him about her dreams? Those were dreams that she'd held inside her heart. They were *sacred*. Now those dreams felt tainted by Hunter's ludicrous plan. Rylee just wanted to be away from him. Why had she agreed to work for him in the first place? He was just like every other man with money, thinking he could buy his way through life.

"I promise you, that's not true. I just found out about this at the meeting this morning. Last night, I was honestly interested in learning more about you. I still am."

She glared at him and shook her head in disbelief before turning to head back up the shore. She was determined to gather her things and leave quickly, but she could feel him following closely behind her.

"Listen, I know what it's like to grow up with a parent who is working all the time." His words stopped her dead in her tracks. What was that supposed to mean? Was he comparing her to his father? She turned to face him, ready to give him a piece of her mind.

Before she could speak, he continued. "I can tell that you love your son dearly and you want to spend more time with him. I can make that possible for you and Liam. You could have all the time in the world to spend with your son if you didn't have to work multiple jobs. This is a win-win for both of us, and Liam deserves it. So do you." He took a step closer. "I'm not trying to buy you;

it's a business deal—just between us—designed to give us both what we want."

His words cut through her. It was enough that Liam had to grow up without a father, but she hated that he was growing up with a mother who was always at work. He spent more time at daycare and with her parents than he did with her and that killed her. She would love to spend more time with her son and this might be a way for that to happen. As angry as the offer made her, she had to think of Liam.

"And you think fifty grand is going to make it so I don't have to work multiple jobs?" Fifty grand sounded like a lot of money to her, but she was wise enough to know that wouldn't go far after she opened her dance studio and paid all the start-up fees. She'd already done the research.

"You're right. Would one hundred thousand dollars do it? I happen to know there's a commercial space for lease in town that would be perfect for your studio. I know the listing broker. I'll even set up the meeting for you."

She knew just the space he was speaking of. She'd driven past it several times since it had opened up last month, each time envisioning it as her dance studio. It was perfect, and it was the only space available in town—it wouldn't last. The fact that Hunter knew of the space she'd dreamed of having as her dance studio on numerous occasions had to be a sign. Was everything finally lining up for her?

"What would I have to do if we were to make this deal? What would be expected of me?"

"All you would have to do is pretend to be my fiancée for a couple months. The board is set to make a decision in a month, and then, of course, I don't want them to see I've lost my fiancée right away. You'd just need to attend a few company events, maybe a family dinner or two, and be seen together around town a bit."

She considered his words. Could she do it? Would she have *time* to do it? Free time was not something she had much of.

"Of course, you'll need to quit your other jobs," Hunter said, as if reading her mind.

"No way. I need my jobs." She shook her head, deciding that would be a deal breaker.

"You won't need them when all is said and done, but if it makes you feel better, then ask for a temporary leave of absence."

She considered that idea for a moment. That felt better than quitting. Could that work? But what if this fell through? Avery would probably approve the leave, but she wasn't so sure about Ripples. What would she tell them her reason was? This was a lot to consider.

"When would I get paid?"

"How about twenty percent up front and the remaining balance in eight weeks?"

She turned to face the water to do the calculation. Twenty percent up front would be twenty grand. That was more than enough to pay her cost of living, send Liam to camp, and perhaps secure the lease on the studio.

"What about my family? I wouldn't feel right lying to them. What about Avery?"

"No, you could tell no one about our arrangement. That's too risky. Especially Avery. She's marrying my brother."

Rylee let out a long sigh and stared out at the water.

"Of course, you'll need to wear a ring, which we can shop for together."

"That's not necessary. It's a business deal, and I won't have any attachment to the ring. Whatever you pick out will be fine."

Hunter's eyes lit up with hope. "So, we have a deal?" He held out his hand for a shake.

She turned back to him and hesitated. She was shocked at herself for even considering saying yes. But she would do anything to give Liam a better life, and this was an opportunity of a lifetime. Plus, it was only for two months. How bad could it possibly be?

She returned his handshake, and a charge passed between them. "We have a deal."

Hunter couldn't believe she had agreed. That was easier than he'd imagined. One hundred grand was a small price to pay if it meant it secured his future as president of Knox Enterprises, but this didn't mean it was a done deal just yet. They still had a lot of work to do to convince everyone that they were in love.

First things first, he went upstairs to his home office to call his attorney. They needed a contract, and he'd better have her sign a nondisclosure agreement as well. He couldn't let this plan get leaked; that would ruin everything. Her confidentiality would be mandatory or the contract would be null and void. His lawyer would definitely need to add that in.

In less than an hour, his lawyer had prepared and emailed the paperwork, which he was in the process of printing when he heard a knock on his office door.

"Come in," he said from his glass desk that faced a wall of floor-to-ceiling windows.

Rylee entered to his left, and he turned to greet her.

"I've finished up for the day, and I'll be leaving soon. I need to work my shift at Ripples this evening. I can't leave them short-handed without notice, but I will speak with my boss tonight and tell him I need a leave of absence, like you suggested."

She didn't look happy and that tugged at his conscience, but he was making her an offer of a lifetime, one that would give her and her son a better life. He just had to keep reminding himself of that.

"Very good," he said, standing to retrieve the paperwork from the printer behind him. "Before you go, I just need you to sign these. I have your first check for you as well." He pulled his checkbook out of the top drawer of the filing cabinet next to the printer.

Rylee sat on the edge of the chair across from his desk and studied the paperwork he'd placed in front of her.

"The first is our contract, with the stipulations outlined as we discussed. The second is an NDA which protects my assets should you leak our plan to the public."

"Why would I do that? You think I want anyone to know I've agreed to this crazy plan of yours?"

"Well, I have to protect myself, and you should note line thirteen before you sign. If you break confidentiality in any way, the contract is null and void, and you will not receive your final payment. Is that understood?"

"Like I said," she told him through gritted teeth. "I'm not going to tell anyone."

"Even Avery? I know she's a good friend of yours, but you must understand, her fiancé is my brother, and although he's not close to the family, I can't have this getting back to my father under any circumstances. Do I have your word?"

"You have it in writing," she said quietly as she picked up the pen and signed both pages.

Was that annoyance he detected in her voice? Or sadness? Shouldn't she be happy he was about to write her a check for twenty thousand dollars? She really was different than any other woman he'd ever met. He'd put a lot on her for one day, so he couldn't blame her if she was upset. Was she having second thoughts? If so, it didn't really matter now. She had signed the paperwork and it was a done deal.

He had himself a fiancée. Now, he just needed a ring.

CHAPTER 7

*M*onday morning came and Rylee was scheduled at Arbor Shores Resort for her cleaning shift. Her plan was to talk to Avery about taking some time off while she was there, but she still wasn't exactly sure what she would say. It wouldn't be as easy as it had been telling Ripples last night. While her boss wasn't happy to lose her for a month in the height of their busy summer season, he also didn't pry when she told him she had some family issues she needed to deal with, and he approved the leave without much fuss. Avery, on the other hand, knew Rylee inside and out, and would know something was up. What was she going to tell her best friend? As close to the truth as possible without exposing her arrangement with Hunter. That was the plan.

First things first, she had to deposit Hunter's check in the bank. It was making her nervous to carry around a check so large. She'd never even seen a check for twenty thousand dollars before, much less had one made out to her. She didn't want to deposit it in the branch in town. What if someone recognized her and started asking questions? She couldn't risk anyone seeing it was written from Hunter Knox. That might tip off their plan. Even though the bank was sworn to confidentiality, she couldn't take a chance of anyone finding out, and in a town this small, good news traveled fast. After she dropped Liam off at daycare, she drove far outside of town and deposited it in a branch in the city.

Rylee rushed back to Arbor Shores as quickly as possible, but made it to the resort fifteen minutes late for her shift. It was unlike her to be late; she prided herself on her punctuality. Her plan was to slip inside, and get started cleaning, then find Avery after her shift ended. No such luck. When she approached the employee entrance of the resort, Avery was right there waiting at the back door, a concerned look on her face.

"Oh, good, you're here." Avery put her arm around Rylee and began walking with her to the time clock. "I was starting to worry about you. I don't think you've ever once been late to work. Everything okay?"

"Um, yeah. I just got held up this morning … in traffic." It wasn't exactly a lie, the traffic in the city had been horrible.

"Traffic in Arbor Shores?" Avery asked with a laugh. The only time their small northern town saw any traffic was on the weekends when vacationers would come up from downstate or during the holiday weekends. Never on a Monday morning.

"There must've been an accident or something." Rylee grabbed her time sheet from the hanger on the wall and stamped it before putting it back in its place. Telling Avery was going to be harder than she'd expected.

"It doesn't matter, I'm just glad you're here. I want to get your opinion on something. I'm trying to decide on colors for the wedding. I have swatches laid out in my office. Come look."

"Great, I'll come take a look after my shift." Rylee wasn't ready to be alone with Avery. Their talk was inevitable, but she wanted to buy more time.

"Don't be silly. Those rooms can wait. We don't have many guests checking in today anyway. Everyone is still checking out from the weekend. Come on." Avery grabbed her hand and pulled her toward the office. Rylee could tell her friend was excited, so she gave in.

"Think winter wonderland," Avery said once they made their way to the office, holding up an evergreen color swatch. "What do you think of this green?"

Rylee wrinkled her nose and shook her head.

"Okay, what about this crimson red?" She held up another swatch.

"I like that better," Rylee agreed, but her head wasn't into it.

"Is everything okay, Ry?" Avery asked, dropping the swatches on the desk. "You're not yourself today."

"Actually, I need to talk to you about something."

Avery took a seat in the chair behind the desk, a look of concern on her face. She nodded at the chair across from her, motioning for Rylee to sit. "Of course. What is it?"

"I-I need to take some time off from the resort, if that's okay? It should only be for a month or so. Well, two months actually." Rylee studied the string from her hoodie that she was twisting around her finger.

"Can you afford to do that? I mean, you were just looking for extra work last week, and now you want to give up your shifts here?"

Good point. "Well, Hunter has offered me a full-time job for the rest of summer." Again, it wasn't a lie. It just wasn't the whole truth.

"That dirty rat!" Avery scoffed. "I recommended you for a couple of cleaning shifts, and then he goes and steals you from me!"

"He's offered to pay me quite a bit. Enough that I won't have to work at Ripples, and I can get more time with Liam before he leaves for camp."

"You're going to quit Ripples?"

"Actually, they approved a leave of absence, so I haven't exactly quit."

"Wow, he must really be paying you well. But why is it only temporary?"

She had to think fast. "Well, he had hired someone else, but she can't start until fall. With the money he's paying me, I'll be able to send Liam to camp and possibly open my dance studio. Or at least secure the lease."

"Well, I know that's your dream, but are you ready for all of that? I mean, will you be able to afford it? Even with a full-time salary from Hunter?"

"There's a space in town I want to see about leasing. There's not much overhead in a dance studio. I've been doing my research. I think I can get it going with relatively low start-up costs."

"Really? That's great! It's just so sudden."

"You have the resort and Emma has NovelTea Books. It just had me thinking lately it's time for me to get moving on my own dreams. I can't wait tables forever."

"You work harder than anyone I know. If anyone deserves this, it's you." Avery flashed a genuine smile. "I'm proud of you, Ry."

"It's a good opportunity for Liam and me. So, if I could take some time off, that would be helpful." She finally looked up and met her friend with hopeful eyes.

"Well, I did just hire someone new. I'm sure she would like the extra shifts. I don't see why that would be a problem."

Rylee let out a long breath as relief washed over her. That had gone better than expected. She got up and moved around the desk to give Avery a hug.

Avery stood to embrace her friend, but after a moment, she took a step back and studied Rylee with a suspicious look. "You're sure nothing else is going on?"

A lump formed in Rylee's throat. "I'm sure."

"Promise?" Avery held out her pinky and waited for Rylee to lock fingers, something they had been doing since they were kids.

Rylee took her friend's pinky in hers and forced a smile. "Promise."

She didn't want to hold things back from Avery, but she had no other choice.

Hunter left his office in the city around lunchtime; he had something important to do.

He pulled into Harry Winston and parked out back. They were expecting him and buzzed him in through the back door. A large man dressed in a black suit escorted him to a private office where the jeweler was awaiting his arrival.

"Mr. Knox, welcome." The jeweler stood to shake his hand. "Can we get you something to drink? Champagne perhaps?"

"That won't be necessary. This won't take long." He took a seat across from the jeweler.

Rylee had said any ring would do, so he didn't plan to put much thought into it. His plan was to get something big enough to grab attention, and get this over with.

"We've taken the liberty of pulling some of our most exquisite pieces for you to view." The man placed a black cloth on the table between them and flipped on the light to showcase the first diamond ring, which he held up by long tweezers.

"This one is four carats. The diamond is a flawless cushion cut and the setting, of course, is platinum. You'll notice—"

"I'll take it." Hunter cut the man off before he could continue with the description. It was just what he had envisioned, and it would do the trick.

The jeweler stifled a chuckle. "Surely you'd like to see the other rings first. It takes time to make a decision of this magnitude for your lady."

"I don't need to see anything else." Hunter pulled out his wallet and tossed a black American Express card on the table between them.

"Mr. Knox, with all due respect, you haven't even asked the price."

"The price is irrelevant. Wrap it up, please." He was growing annoyed now and the jeweler must have sensed it.

Without another word, the jeweler pulled a ring box out of the drawer and gave the diamond one final polish. "Excellent choice, Mr. Knox. You must have a very special lady to deserve such a beautiful ring."

A vision of Rylee flashed through Hunter's mind and he stifled a grin.

Special she was, indeed.

When Rylee's shift ended at the resort, she took a sigh of relief that things had gone so well with Avery, but she figured she'd better call Hunter and inform him of what she had told her, in case Shane got to him first.

When she got into her car, she pulled her cell out of her purse and grabbed the card he had given her from his wallet. She studied it for a moment. *Hunter Knox, Vice President, Knox Enterprises*, with a slew of numbers. Which one should she call? It was Monday morning so he was most likely at work, so perhaps she should call the office? Better yet, if she called his cell and he didn't answer, she could just leave a voicemail and wouldn't have to speak with him. A much better plan. She punched in his cell number and waited, praying he wouldn't pick up.

"Hunter Knox," he answered on the third ring.

She cleared her throat. "Hi, it's Rylee."

"Rylee, I was just thinking about you."

"I just wanted to let you know I talked to Avery today and I thought maybe we should go over what I said. You know, in case Shane or anyone asks any questions."

"Good thinking. Let's have dinner tonight."

"Tonight?" That's not what she'd expected. "That's really not necessary. I can just tell you over the phone."

"Actually, we have a lot to discuss. Does seven o'clock work for you?"

"No, actually, I don't have a sitter tonight for Liam. My parents do bingo on Mondays, so I'm afraid this isn't a good night for me."

Silence filled the other end of the line while she waited for a response.

"Bring him," he finally said. "How about 7 p.m.? My place. See you then." And with that, the other line went dead. He had hung up before she could offer a rebuttal. *The nerve of him.* Was he used to always getting his way? If they were going to make this work for a couple of months, some things would need to change.

As she drove to the daycare to get Liam, she started to worry about how her son was going to take to all of this. He was seven now and extremely bright. It's not like she could hide a relationship with Hunter from him. How were they going to discuss logistics in front of him? She didn't like the idea of taking Liam with her, especially after the way Hunter had acted the first time he'd met Liam, but she had no choice.

While Liam was getting cleaned up, she took a quick shower and then scanned her closet for something to wear. It was looking bleak. Perhaps she could take some of the money he had paid her and get some new clothes. She hated to spend money on herself, but she didn't have many options for going out, and she'd have a few events to attend with Hunter. Luckily, tonight she was just going to his house for dinner, so she settled on her best pair of blue jeans, a sleeveless beige blouse, and brown sandals.

She gave herself a once-over in her full-length mirror and scrunched at her curls. Not one for much makeup, she took a moment to dab some gloss on her lips and put a coat of mascara on her lashes before she headed to the kitchen to find Liam. "Ready, buddy?"

"Where are we going again?" he asked, without breaking concentration from the picture he was drawing.

"To Mr. Knox's house. Remember Shane's brother?"

"The man with the big house who doesn't like kids? Why are we going *there*?"

It was a fair question. One in which she didn't have an immediate answer.

"Don't be silly, Liam. Mr. Knox likes kids." But did he? Her son was more receptive than she thought.

"Can I bring my sketch pad and pencils?" He looked up at her, a frown on his face. Her heart broke. She hated involving him in this.

"Of course." *Let's just remember to put something under it this time.* Rylee blew out a long breath and they headed for the door.

CHAPTER 8

*H*unter answered the door dressed for a night out. He greeted Rylee with a smile and then noticed she was in jeans. Sure, she looked great in a casual way, but this would never do for the evening he had planned. That's why he'd had his assistant shop for a dress earlier that day.

His eyes quickly fell to Liam. He had some making up to do after their last encounter, but he wasn't particularly good with kids. It's not that he didn't like them, he just wasn't ever around them much. None of his brothers had children, and as the youngest Knox, he was the end of the line.

"Hi, Liam." He kneeled down to greet the young boy at his level.

"Hiya, Mr. Knox," Liam said, looking at his own feet.

"How about you call me Hunter?"

"Okay," Liam agreed, without looking up.

"I have a surprise for you."

Liam met his eyes with a hint of excitement. "For me? What is it?"

"Follow me." Hunter headed for the dining room table and the boy followed. He had placed a tablecloth down to protect the wood, and had taken the liberty of buying every art supply a kid could ever dream of.

"Wow! What's all this?" Liam's eyes were wide as saucers and Hunter beamed. Perhaps he might've finally done something right.

"This is for you. I didn't know what all you like, so I just got a little of everything."

Liam took a seat at the table and started picking up brushes and colored pencils to inspect them.

"What do you say, Liam?" Rylee asked.

"Thank you, Mr. Kn—I mean, Hunter."

"You're welcome." Hunter watched the wonder in the boy's eyes and took a moment to revel in the joy that came from doing something nice, followed by a pang of sadness that rippled through him. He thought about his own childhood, and how he'd always loved to write as a young boy. But nobody had ever paid attention to his passions as a child. Had someone taken an interest, who knows what might have happened. He might have a book published by now. If he could make a difference in this boy's life during their short time together, perhaps that would somehow make up for not following his own childhood dreams.

The sound of the doorbell echoed through the massive estate, breaking him from his thoughts.

"Is someone joining us?" Rylee asked.

"No, that's the sitter." Hunter headed toward the door.

"Excuse me?" Rylee called after him. She didn't sound happy, but he'd already arranged for the sitter, and Liam would be occupied with his art all evening anyway.

What was coming next needed to be done in public, and he'd already decided tonight was the night.

∾

When the front door opened, Rylee silently seethed. Who was this young girl, and why did Hunter think it was okay to hire a sitter for her son without consulting her first? She was already feeling uncomfortable about all of this, and Hunter was not making things any easier.

"Becca, come in. I want you to meet someone," he said, greeting the young girl with long blonde hair that reached her behind and a shirt that seemed a bit too low cut. She looked like she was dressed for a night out with her girlfriends, not an evening of babysitting.

"Hey, Mr. Knox." She followed him in, all smiles. As they got closer, Rylee fought with all her might to control her temper.

"Rylee, this is Becca Edwards. She's an intern at the office. She loves children and has two younger brothers of her own, so she's excited to get to know Liam." He turned to Becca. "Becca, this is Rylee."

"Hunter, may I speak to you privately for a moment?" Rylee asked, without addressing the girl. It wasn't like her to be rude, but she was not pleased with the situation Hunter had orchestrated.

"Okay, but we have to be quick. We have reservations at the yacht club in fifteen minutes. Becca, Liam is in the dining room if you'd like to go introduce yourself," he said before leading Rylee out back.

As soon as the glass door slid closed and they were out of earshot of Becca, Rylee erupted. "How dare you hire a sitter for my son without asking me first." Her temper was at an all-time high, but she fought to keep her voice low.

"You can trust Becca. I assure you, she is experienced and loves children. Liam will be fine with her for a couple of hours."

"That's beside the point. You never asked me if it was okay. You just assumed. And I thought we were coming here for dinner.

I didn't know we were going out, and I'm not dressed for the yacht club."

She'd never even been to the Arbor Shores Yacht Club, but she was sure her blue jeans and sandals were not going to make the cut. Especially by the looks of what Hunter was wearing. He had on dark gray slacks, with a long-sleeved, black button-down shirt tucked into them. He looked handsome as ever and Rylee suddenly felt uncomfortable and underdressed. She folded her arms in front of her and glared at Hunter, waiting for an explanation.

"You are right, I should have told you. But don't worry, I have it handled. There's a dress and shoes waiting for you upstairs in the guest room." He'd gone shopping for her? Did he think she was unable to dress herself for dinner at the yacht club? She was sure she'd never been more insulted. She tried to recall if there was a clause in the agreement that would allow her to get out of this deal. She'd made a huge mistake agreeing to this plan.

Hunter took a step toward her and placed a hand on her arm. "Listen, I'm sorry. I should've communicated with you. It's just that we have a lot to discuss, and I didn't think you'd want to do so in front of Liam. Plus, we need to be seen in public together. That was part of our deal."

She looked down at his hand on her arm, wondering why he was touching her. He swiftly removed it, but she could still feel his hand there. The warmth of his touch had soothed her. Or was it his apology? Either way, she was starting to calm down.

"We are going to have to set some ground rules." She looked up at him. "First, plans need to be discussed with me so I know what's going on."

"Not a problem. It won't happen again." He slipped his hands into his pockets and nodded.

"Second, I make *all* decisions for my son. Not you."

"Got it."

"Third, I can dress myself. After tonight, I'm going to need to go shopping before we have anymore outings like this, so I'd appreciate a list of everything you have planned for us so that I know what to buy."

"Noted. I'll call to set you up an appointment with a stylist first thing tomorrow morning."

A stylist? She was sure she could pick out her own clothes, but she would let that one go for now.

"Now, can you please go get changed so we can get to dinner? We're going to be late for our reservation." Hunter made a praying motion with his hands, and something about his hopeful grin made the butterflies in her stomach begin to flutter. He had the sexiest of smiles, and she had to take a moment to remind herself that she was upset with him.

Without answering, she started walking toward the house. She needed to make sure Liam was okay with this first. She shouldn't have brought him, much less be leaving him alone with a stranger. This was going to be two long months, and so far, things were not off to a good start.

CHAPTER 9

*H*unter pulled his black Ferrari in front of the Yacht Club and waited for the valet to open Rylee's door. He figured bringing out the sports car was the fastest way to get everyone's attention, and tonight he needed all eyes on them.

The Knoxes were long-standing members of the yacht club, and even though his father might not be there on a Monday night, nothing would happen at the club without Carter Knox finding out about it. This was the perfect place for Hunter to carry out his plan.

"Good evening, Mr. Knox," the valet driver greeted him as he exited the vehicle. Hunter nodded and handed over the key fob as he made his way to the curb to meet Rylee.

Rylee was breathtaking in the black cocktail dress his assistant had picked out. But why did she seem so upset that he had a dress picked out for her? Her independence confused him, but it lit a fire inside of him at the same time. In the best possible way.

"Ready?" He greeted her with a smile and put his hand on the small of her back to guide her toward the door. She looked uncomfortable, but he could understand that. Had she ever even been to the yacht club before? He doubted it.

"Mr. Knox, lovely to see you," Maggie, the hostess, greeted him with a kiss to both cheeks, gussied up in her usual style— silver hair pulled back into a tight bun and enough makeup caked on to age her at least ten extra years. Tonight, she was dressed in a black beaded gown. He always thought she dressed more like a lounge singer than a hostess, but that was Maggie for you.

"We have a lovely waterside table set up for you out on the veranda." She grabbed two menus from the hostess stand while giving Rylee a once-over.

Hunter cleared his throat, and Maggie snapped her attention in his direction. "Something inside the lounge would be better," he told her.

He had originally made the reservation for a waterside table, but he could see that tonight the lounge was already filling up with members. Tony, the club's pianist, played the piano softly in the corner next to the bar that ran the length of the room. Men in dinner jackets lined the bar and drank cordials from snifters while their wives sipped wine and chatted amongst themselves. It was a scene he knew well; he'd practically grown up here, after all.

Hunter was known as the club's young bachelor. But tonight, he was going to join the men's club.

Rylee followed the hostess through the room and prayed for a table in the corner, away from all the eyes that were boring holes into her. Women stopped mid-chew to stare as they made their way through the maze of tables in the middle of the room. To Rylee's delight, the hostess seated them at a cozy table to the far right of the room, in front of a picturesque window overlooking the marina. The room was dark, encompassed with mahogany wood and ambient lighting. The view of the setting sun behind the yachts was at least giving her something to focus on so she didn't have to acknowledge the stares and whispers still pointed in their direction. She'd driven by the yacht club and marina a million times, and often wondered what it was like inside. Now she knew she hadn't been missing anything and would've been better off never knowing. These were not her kind of people, that was for sure.

The hostess pulled out her chair and waited for Rylee to be seated before handing her a menu, taking one more opportunity to give her a good hard look before handing Hunter his menu.

"Thank you, Maggie." Hunter took his dinner napkin and placed it in his lap and Rylee followed suit. It wasn't long before the server appeared and took their drink order.

"What's good here?" Rylee finally asked as she perused the menu, breaking the silence between them.

"Monday is prime rib night, but please order anything you'd like. I like the lake perch myself."

She closed her menu and placed it on the table. "Lake perch sounds fine." An amber glow shown through the window and illuminated Hunter's chiseled features. She studied him for a moment. He really was handsome. It was too bad he was just another arrogant rich guy. Great features were always wasted on the ones who had it all.

Shortly thereafter, the waiter delivered their beverages and took their dinner order, leaving them with no menu as a buffer between them and nothing to do but get to know one another.

"Are you doing okay?" he finally asked. Had he noticed how uncomfortable she was? Perhaps it was obvious.

"I"m fine," she replied, taking a sip of her water.

"So, how is it possible I've never met you before? Did you go to school here?"

"We went to school together, but I was in Avery's grade. After high school, I left for New York. I've only been back a short while." She fought to keep her voice low in case the meddling eyes had curious ears as well. "What about you? How long have you worked in the family business?" She was trying to sound interested; she was a good sport and would do her best to live up to her end of this deal, even if it made her wildly uncomfortable to be a participant in his world.

"I went to work in the family business fresh out of high school while I attended Northern University. After college, I started full-time, and the rest is history."

"So, what do you do for fun? I mean, when you're not working?"

"I'm always working," he said with a grin, but she had a feeling he was serious. "But I do love boating. In fact, that one is mine in that slip seven down." He pointed out the window and she wondered if she had the slips counted right. Clearly that massive yacht was not his. What would a single man need with a boat that size? Perhaps he was trying to overcompensate for something else missing in his life.

"You really have it all. The house, the cars, the boat. It seems like you could get any girl to agree to be your fiancée for free." She lowered her voice to a whisper with her final words.

"Yeah, but I'm not great at relationships. It's hard to get close to people when you don't know their true intentions, and you never know if they are interested in you for you or for the wrong reasons." Hunter looked out the window, then quickly added. "Besides, I don't need any romantic complications right now. I just need to focus on acquiring the company."

Something flit across Hunter's face with his words. She looked down and picked at some imaginary lint on the white tablecloth. Was work all he really cared about? Something in his eyes told a different story. Something told her there was more behind that than what he was revealing. It must be awful to wonder if people were interested in you or your money. That's something she'd never had to experience, and never wanted to.

"Plus, it's more fun being here with you," he added.

She looked up and was met with a smile that would give a movie star a run for his money. Where did that come from? Did he really enjoy her company? He barely knew her. Somehow, though, his comment put her at ease, and she was beginning to think there may be more to him than just the stereotypical rich guy she'd labeled him as.

Rylee decided to ignore his last comment. Still, she was oddly intrigued by him, and she was determined to understand Hunter. "So outside of work and boating, what's your real passion?"

"Is this twenty questions?" he asked with a playful grin.

"I'm just trying to get to know you better. Besides, you know my passion. I told you about ballet and my dreams of opening a studio."

"Touché," he took a drink of his cocktail and paused for a moment. Was he trying to figure out something clever to say or was he hesitant to open up? "Actually, I've always loved to write."

"Really?" she asked, trying not to act too shocked but it came out quicker than she'd anticipated.

"Why do you sound so surprised?"

"I don't know. I just didn't picture you as the type."

"Writers have a type?"

"Well, I guess not now that you put it that way. What do you write?"

"Nowadays? Not much other than business proposals and contracts. But when I was growing up, I loved to write short stories. Fiction. Imaginary worlds that take the reader to another place. I always wanted to write a novel."

"So, why haven't you?"

"I don't know. Time, I guess. Or, it could be that I never felt supported in my dreams as a child."

She was amazed at how much he was opening up to her. The

waiter delivered their salads and they both took a few bites before he continued.

"When I was growing up, every year for Christmas I asked for a typewriter, but never got one."

"A typewriter?" she snorted and put down her fork. "You know, we are in the computer age and have been for decades."

"Yeah, but I always wanted an old vintage one, you know?" His eyes lit up. "I could envision myself at my desk just pounding away on that old typewriter, creating my masterpiece." He looked up as if daydreaming about that idea.

"And you never got one?"

"Nope." He snapped back to reality and took one final stab at his salad before pushing it aside. "I asked and asked, probably for every birthday and Christmas as far back as I can remember. But my father refused to support that dream. Even though he had more money than he knew what to do with, he would never buy me that vintage typewriter."

Rylee's heart sank, and she pulled back the desire to reach her hand across the table and console him. Here she thought because he'd come from money that he'd probably never wanted for anything in his life, yet he had parents who didn't support him. She realized how lucky she was. Even though she didn't have much growing up, her parents went out of their way to ensure she got to attend every dance class ever offered. She was grateful for it.

"Why didn't you ever buy one for yourself?"

"I don't know. By the time I was old enough to afford one, I had already decided to squash that dream."

"You didn't squash that dream. Your father did."

Hunter shot a look at her. Had she overstepped her boundaries? She knew how close he was with his father … wasn't he? Perhaps she'd said too much. She looked down at her salad and started separating the shaved carrots from the lettuce.

"You're right," he said softly, almost under his breath. He glanced at his watch and then looked around the room just as the server approached with their main courses. They enjoyed their meal over lighter conversation while they ate.

Hunter excused himself from the table after he ordered their dessert, and Rylee noticed several people trying to stop him as he made his way through the room. He swiftly shook hands but brushed off all conversation until he got to the piano player. He whispered something in his ear. What could he be saying to the pianist?

Hunter returned to the table about the time the waitress brought out a dish of crème brulee for them to share. As she placed it on the table, the pianist began singing and playing "You Look Wonderful Tonight" by Eric Clapton.

"I had him play this for you," he said, looking into her eyes before scooping up a spoonful of the dessert.

"For me? Why?"

"Because you really do look wonderful. I can tell you feel out of place being here. This is my way of saying I'm sorry for not communicating better with you and hiring a sitter for your son."

Heat flushed to her cheeks. Was he trying to charm her? What came next was a complete and utter shock. As the pianist continued to play, he rose to his feet and held out his hand for her.

"No way. I'm not dancing."

"Please, just one dance?"

"I don't want to be in the middle of this room. Not tonight."

"It's part of our deal," he reminded her, still holding out his hand. She took it hesitantly and allowed him to lead her to the middle of the small dance area near the piano. Nobody else was dancing, and silence fell over the room as everyone stopped what they were doing to watch.

When they reached the dance floor, instead of pulling her in for a slow dance, Hunter dropped to his knee and kneeled before her, pulling something from his pocket.

Tell me he's not ...

He reached for her hand and held it softly. The pianist stopped playing so everyone could hear what Hunter was about to say. The room hushed with silence.

"Rylee Benton, since the moment you came into my life, I've known you were the one. Even though we haven't known each other long, I feel like I've known you forever. Will you do me the honor of becoming my wife? If so, you'll make me the happiest man alive."

What was he doing? This wasn't part of the plan. They'd discussed that she would have to wear a ring, but he'd never mentioned a public proposal. He could've at least given her a heads up. Her body flushed with heat, and her knees threatened to give out. Yet, something about his words made her feel special, even if it was all a big lie. Nobody in her life had ever said anything even remotely close to that to her. A medley of anger and embarrassment mixed with emotions of pride and joy inside her. She wasn't sure what she was feeling, but saying no wasn't an option.

She looked down at the ring in the box he held before her. Why would he buy such a beautiful ring for only two month's use? She looked from the ring to his eyes. They looked hopeful with a hint of worry. Did he really think there might be a chance she'd say no? At this point, she was a sure thing even if she was upset that he'd sprung this on her without warning.

"Yes," she whispered, and the entire room started clapping. The pianist resumed playing and Hunter rose to his feet, placing his arms around her waist and pulling her into him. *Was he about to—*

Before she could comprehend what was happening, his hand traveled up her back to the nape of her neck and pulled her mouth to his. Should she pull away? No, she couldn't. She had to act like an excited new fiancée. She had to not only accept the kiss, but make it look as natural as possible. And that wasn't hard to do. His lips were soft, and they tasted so good—the sweetness of the dessert still lingered on them. His strong arms wrapped around her body, causing her to melt into him. She clasped her fingers behind his neck and allowed him to continue to kiss her, the insecure feeling she'd had about the audience watching was now a distant memory.

The whole world went blank as she focused on Hunter's lips on hers and the light scent of his cologne that smelled better than any man she'd ever known. She couldn't remember the last time she'd been kissed, and she was certain she'd never been kissed like this. He made it seem so real.

Applause erupted throughout the room, jolting her back to reality. For a moment, she forgot that it was all a lie.

Until the kiss ended and so did their dinner, and then the sobering reality of their situation began to settle in.

After dinner, Hunter wasn't ready for the evening to end. He'd never meant to kiss her like he did, but now that he had, he was as confused as ever. How was it possible that kissing Rylee could make him feel like this? This wasn't part of the plan.

"It's a nice night. Would you like to see my boat?" he asked as they walked outside the yacht club.

"Sure." She was more receptive than he thought she would be, and that was a good sign. Was she feeling it, too?

He held out his hand to her, and after studying it for a moment, she placed her soft hand in his. It felt so natural there—another thing he wasn't expecting.

Hunter got on the boat first, and then helped Rylee on after she'd slipped her shoes off at the dock. He was impressed that she knew boat etiquette, but where did that come from?

It was dark now, and the moon shone down on the water, casting a silver glow on the harbor.

"Come on, let's go up front," he told her, allowing her to walk ahead of him.

Once at the front of the bow, the light of the moon illuminated her face, and somehow, she was growing even more beautiful by the minute. A gentle breeze blew a long strand of hair across her face, and he reached out to tuck it behind her ear. She looked up at him and held his gaze as he fought with himself on whether or not to kiss her. He wanted nothing more than to feel her lips on his once more, just to see if he had been imagining the chemistry between them, and if, by chance, she felt it, too.

Rylee turned away, as if she sensed what he was about to do, and faced the water. "It's beautiful, Hunter. But really, I should be getting home to Liam."

Perhaps he had been imagining it. She wasn't the slightest bit interested in him. That was clear. From this point on, he'd have to keep it strictly professional and keep a clear head.

That would mean no more kissing.

CHAPTER 10

*H*unter awoke the next morning with thoughts of the prior evening playing over in his head. The night, the proposal—it all couldn't have gone any more perfectly. But the drive back home had been filled with awkward silence. What had come over him? Was that kiss really necessary? Yes, he had to do it to make the whole proposal believable. The element of surprise was imperative. That was the only way to make it seem real, so it would unfold like a true proposal. Hopefully, he hadn't given Rylee the wrong idea. She had to know that was all for show, right? As much as he'd enjoyed it, they had to keep this professional. Love was a complication he didn't have time for right now.

But for show or not, he couldn't deny there was something that just felt right about that kiss. He could still feel her lips on his, and a part of him really liked that. Especially the part where she'd reciprocated. He could've played that moment over in his mind a few more times, but he had to get up and get busy. He had a big day ahead of him, and already he had two missed calls from his father. It appeared as though his plan may have worked.

His phone buzzed again and the screen lit up. It was Carter calling. *Showtime.*

"Hi, Dad."

"Hunter, who is this girl you took to the club last night?"

"That would be my fiancée."

"Oh, yes, I'm well aware of your *antics*."

"My 'antics'? You mean my proposal?"

"From what I understand, you took some girl to the club and asked her to marry you in front of everyone. Where did you meet this girl, anyway?"

"I assure you, Rylee is great, and you'll love her."

"Well, I would have liked a chance to meet her before you introduced her as your fiancée to the entire yacht club."

Heat rose up inside Hunter as he fought to keep his cool. He knew better than to stand up to his father. He expected, or at least hoped, his father would show the slightest bit of excitement for him, but no. All Carter seemed to worry about was social status and what people would think. He should've known.

"I want to meet this girl. Bring her by the house tomorrow night."

"Yes, sir." What was it about his father that still made him do whatever he said? This was a critical time, and he had to show his father he was ready to settle down, yet part of him would just like to tell him off sometimes. But that's something he had never done and never would. Was it respect? Fear? Or a combination of both? Whatever it was, Carter Knox held Hunter's fate in his hands, and Hunter would do whatever he had to do to make sure Knox Enterprises was his.

And right now, that meant making over Rylee before this plan went any further.

~

Rylee dropped Liam off at daycare and headed to Hunter's. The last thing he'd told her the night before was to be at his house by 9 a.m. She assumed that meant to clean. Part of her was frustrated that he expected her to be his fiancée *and* his maid, but without working at the resort and Ripples, she'd be bored otherwise, so she didn't mind too much.

She pulled down his long driveway to find he still had that dang Ferrari parked out front. Man, she disliked that car. She never saw the use for such flashy, extravagant purchases, and she'd never felt as out of place as she had getting out of that car last night at the yacht club.

She found the front door ajar as she approached the estate. "Hello," she called through the open door as she made her way inside.

"Good morning," Hunter was standing at the kitchen island with a grin on his face and a coffee cup in hand. He was reading the paper dressed in a white polo shirt that accentuated his tanned arms and a nice pair of jeans. He didn't look like he was headed to the office. This was a look she wasn't used to seeing on him but one she could get used to. He looked more relaxed than he had last night.

"Morning." She did her best to try on a smile, but she was still upset about the public proposal. She was blindsided by the entire evening. Didn't he have any regard for her feelings?

"Ready?" he asked.

"Ready for what?"

"I told you I was going to call first thing this morning and set you up with a stylist. Well, everything is set." He rinsed his cup out in the sink and put it in the dishwasher. "We are due at the airport in one hour."

"The airport? I can't leave town. I have a son to take care of, remember?" Frustration flooded through her. When was he going to stop springing things on her like this?

"We'll be back this afternoon."

"What? No." She shook her head, not willing to entertain his idea. "I can go shopping on my own."

He looked her up and down and raised an eyebrow at her statement. She crossed her arms in front of her body. She had managed to underdress, yet again. Here she was in shorts and a tank top, ready for a day of cleaning.

"The least I can do is take you shopping. Your money is your money. I think of this as a business expense." He flashed a grin at her as he fetched his keys from the dining room table and motioned toward the door.

"But I'm not prepared. I thought I was coming here to clean."

"To clean?" he chuckled. "Why on earth would I have you clean? You're my fiancée now. You don't clean. I'll hire someone else for that."

"Technically, I'm not really your fiancée, and I don't mind the cleaning. It will give me something to do."

"Technically, you are." He motioned to the rock on her finger. "Don't worry, I'll keep you plenty busy." He smiled and moved toward her to guide her in the direction of the door. She could feel his hand on her back and memories of last night on the dance floor flashed through her mind. Chills ran through her body at the thought of that kiss and the moment Hunter placed his lips on hers.

"Where are we going?"

"You'll see." He still had that grin and it was starting to irk her, sexy as it was.

She stopped when they reached the door. "You promise I'll be back by four? That's the latest I can get Liam from daycare."

"I promise."

She did need some new clothes, and as careless as this plan made her feel, a small part of her was enticed by it all. Where was he taking her? She followed him outside and stopped on the front step.

"You coming?" he turned and asked.

"Can't we just take your SUV?"

"Uh, ok. But may I ask why?"

"It's just … I like it better. It's more comfortable."

He stood for a moment smiling at her, as if amused. "Sure thing." He punched a code on the keypad next to the garage door and it opened, revealing the Range Rover inside. She let out a sigh of relief.

Hunter backed the SUV out of the garage and leaned over the passenger seat to open her door. *At least he's a gentleman.* She could have sworn she heard him chuckle to himself as she got in the vehicle.

"What's so funny?"

"Nothing." His eyes lit up in amusement as he watched her.

"Come on, what is it?"

"It's just that I've never quite met a girl like you. That's all."

"What's that supposed to mean?"

He shifted into drive and started down the driveway. "Not many women would pick an SUV over a Ferrari, if you know what I mean."

"Well, I don't know what kind of women you're used to dating, but I beg to differ."

He flashed her a smile and flipped on the radio. Forty minutes later, they were on a jet.

CHAPTER 11

"*I*s this *your* jet?" Rylee asked as she made herself comfortable in the plush leather seat across from Hunter. The seats were positioned to face each other, not side by side like on the commercial flights she was used to.

He sat back in his seat and eyed her with that same amused look on his face she was getting used to seeing on him. Did he get some kind of pleasure from making her feel out of place?

"It's the company's jet."

She took in her surroundings. White leather seats, white carpeting, polished oak tables, and brass finishes. She'd never seen anything like it, except in movies. As nice as it was, was it really necessary? Surely, they could've gone shopping locally.

An attendant appeared from the back. "Good morning, Mr. Knox." She nodded to him and smiled wide at Rylee, placing mimosas in front of each of them.

"Good morning, Susan. This is Rylee Benton."

"Good morning, Ms. Benton." The attendant gave her a genuine smile. "We'll be taking off shortly. That will put us on the ground in approximately 30 minutes. It's a beautiful day in Chicago, the weather is 77 degrees with clear skies."

"Thank you." He nodded and dismissed her.

"Chicago, huh?" Rylee arched a brow at Hunter once the attendant had walked away. Then leaned forward and whispered in a playful tone, "You know, I think they have clothing stores in Traverse City."

"Chicago has the best shopping. And pizza. We'll have lunch before we return."

"Hmm, I don't know," she teased. "New York pizza is hands down the best on earth."

"I predict you'll change your mind before the day is through."

"We'll see about that." She smiled at him for the first time today. Although she wasn't happy about his choices last night, he'd been nothing but a gentleman to her. The least she could do was be polite, especially after he'd gone out of his way to set up this day of shopping for her. On his dime, no less. As uncomfortable as it made her to have him buy her clothes, she'd hate to have to spend her own money on clothes she may never wear again after this fake relationship ended.

She leaned back in her seat and took a sip of her mimosa. She wasn't much of a drinker, but she thought it might loosen her up a bit. Again, she found herself feeling underdressed and out of place, and here she was on a jet of all things in her jean shorts and Keds. Not exactly what she had envisioned for her Tuesday.

Ah, well, when in Rome.

Hunter took a seat on the velvet couch in the private dressing room at Monroe's, a high-end boutique on Michigan Avenue in the heart of downtown Chicago. Monroe's was known for its stylists, and Hunter had flown to Chicago a time or two to have suits tailored there himself. But today was all about Rylee. Janae, her stylist for the day, had taken her measurements as soon as they'd arrived and had already pulled a variety of looks for Rylee to try.

Hunter used his smart phone to work while Rylee tried on clothes. He'd let her know she needed several casual daytime looks for barbecues and summer parties, along with some cocktail dresses for evenings out, and a few gowns for the nicer parties such as the company's gala that Saturday night. That was the most important event, so she had to look the part.

She'd tried on the casual outfits first, and he took a break from his phone to watch her as she'd come out from behind the curtain to study herself in the mirror. She was choosing great outfits, and it was apparent she did have good taste when given the proper options. Now, she was trying on the gowns, and soon they would be finished and could have a bit of fun in Chicago before they headed back.

He heard the curtain to her dressing room slide open and he looked up from his phone to find Rylee standing before him in a formfitting, floor length, strapless black dress with a slit up the left leg that showed off her incredibly toned thigh.

He swallowed hard and took a sip of his water, fighting to act nonchalant. But she was breathtaking. She'd let her hair down, and her full mane of wild curls cascaded over her bare shoulders.

He let out a low whistle. "Wow." Was all he could manage to get out.

"Do you like it?" she asked, with an uncertain look on her face as she turned to the left and right in the mirror to get a view of all angles.

"Do I like it? That's an understatement." He took another sip of his water to avoid choking on that lump in his throat. "Rylee, you look stunning."

They locked eyes for a moment, and he could see her face begin to redden. He was sure his cheeks adorned the same rosy hue. He didn't know what had come over him to make him so forward, but he couldn't help himself. She looked beautiful and she deserved to know it.

"Should I get this one?" she asked.

"That's up to you. I want you to select your own clothes. But if you ask me, you have a winner there."

She tried on a few cocktail dresses and looked like a ten in every one. He couldn't be more pleased with his decision to make Rylee his fiancée. If he had to pretend with anyone, he was glad it was her. There was something refreshing about her, and he was beginning to enjoy having her around. Perhaps the next couple of months wouldn't be so bad after all.

"Mr. Knox, shall I pull more options?" Janae asked when Rylee went back behind the curtain to remove the gown. "So far she's selected seven causal looks, four cocktail dresses, two evening gowns, three purses, and six pairs of shoes."

"I think that's good for one day. Have her wear one of the casual outfits out of here if she'd like. We'll have the rest sent to the jet. We're going to spend some time in Chicago before we leave."

"Very well. It's a beautiful day for it, sir. And you have a beautiful fiancée to show off around town." She smiled warmly, and Hunter beamed. He wondered if he'd ever have a true fiancée on his arm. Well, at least he had Rylee for the time being. Something about her made him want to show her a good time. He had a feeling she deserved it.

He signed the five-figure charge slip and a few minutes later, Rylee emerged in a new outfit. She wore a floral summer dress that fell mid-thigh and strappy white sandals. She had a new Coach clutch under one arm, and she'd pulled her hair back loosely, with wild tendrils escaping in all the right places.

"What is it?" She followed his gaze and looked down at her

body, smoothing an imaginary wrinkle from her dress. "Is something wrong?"

She must've caught him staring, but he was in awe of her. Ever since that kiss last night he was beginning to see her in a different light. Don't even get him started on that kiss. He had to keep reminding himself, it was all pretend. Yet something about it just felt … right.

"It's nothing. You look great." He stood and held out his hand to her. "Ready to go have the best slice of pizza of your life?"

She looked down at his hand, and then placed her hand in his. "I hope this pizza knows it has some big shoes to fill. I'll always be a New York pizza girl at heart."

"We'll see about that." He winked and gave her hand a light squeeze. He was dying to show her a good time, and was thrilled that she would actually eat pizza, not just a salad like the girls he was used to going out with.

As much as Rylee loved Arbor Shores, she'd always been drawn to the energy of a city; that's what had lured her to New York in the first place. So being in Chicago on this beautiful summer day, with the sun shining through the skyscrapers and cabs honking, had her mood on high. She was actually having fun with Hunter, and the shopping wasn't as bad as she thought it would be. She was feeling a bit uncomfortable that he'd paid for it all. She expected he'd spent in excess of twenty grand, and nobody had ever spent that kind of money on her before. But like he said, it was a business expense, so she was trying not to think of it as anything else.

After strolling down Michigan Avenue, and popping into a few more stores along the way, they made their way to Willis

Tower. Hunter insisted she see the view from the top, and he seemed to find pleasure in showing her around the city and watching her reaction to all the fun places he loved in Chicago. Since he had a connection at Willis Tower, they were able to skip the line and get a behind-the-scenes tour.

Up top at the Skydeck, Rylee's jaw dropped in amazement. She'd never seen a sight like this in New York.

"Come on; you have to walk out on the ledge," he told her, and grabbed her hand to guide her.

"The ledge? I don't like the sound of that." She stopped walking and pulled him back toward her. Would this be a good time to tell him she had a slight fear of heights? Nothing debilitating, but she didn't want to be on the ledge of any building, that was for sure.

"The ledge is a glass enclosure that extends four feet off the building, allowing you to see the city below. You'll love it."

Reluctantly, she allowed him to guide her to the glass. She squeezed her eyes shut tight as she inched onto its base.

"Don't worry, I won't let go of you. You're safe," he whispered in her ear, and she could feel his strong arms wrap around her waist from behind as he held her close.

Panic shot through her body. She was sure he could hear her heart pounding in her chest. "I'm afraid to look!" she squealed as she buried her face in her hands.

He pulled her in even tighter and she could feel the warmth of his body behind her. Something about being wrapped in his arms made her feel safe. "Open your eyes. I promise, you're safe with me," he whispered again.

Rylee slowly pulled her hands from her face and opened her eyes. She glanced down quickly and her stomach dropped, causing her to lose her breath. She knew she wouldn't be able to do that again, so she focused on the view of the cityscape on the horizon. "Wow, I bet you can see all the way to Michigan from up here," she said.

"On a clear day, you can see about 50 miles out."

Hunter was still holding her tight, so tight that his warm breath on her ear was making the hair on the back of her neck stand on end.

"It really is spectacular." She turned her head to look over her shoulder at him, and noticed his face was only inches from hers. Her eyes fell to his lips, and a strong desire to once again feel his mouth on hers washed over her. She willed herself to look away, but her eyes met his and were locked.

Still holding her in his arms and her eyes in his gaze, Hunter had a look of hunger about him that she hadn't seen before. Was he going to kiss her? Her eyes began to drift shut and her lips parted.

"Excuse us." A voice beside them jolted her back to reality as two girls who had moved to the glass enclosure squeezed in next to them.

Hunter loosened his grip on Rylee's body and grabbed her hand instead, guiding her back toward the elevator. Just as quickly as she thought they were about to kiss, the moment was over. They were better off. Neither of them needed to go down that road. Hunter had said so himself last night. He didn't need the added distraction of a relationship. That's why he'd made this deal with her in the first place. And she'd sworn off guys like Hunter long ago, so no more romantic encounters with her hot, fake fiancé.

After leaving Willis Tower, they finally found their way to the pizza place down a side road, off the main strip.

"This place has the best pizza in the city," Hunter leaned in and whispered to Rylee as they waited for the hostess to seat them.

She believed it. The place looked like it'd been around for

centuries. The walls were filled with old black and white photos, telling her it had likely been family-owned for generations. In back, you could hear the banter in the kitchen as the open-air window allowed guests to see what was going on from the dining area. The aroma of pizza sauce and Italian seasonings filled the air, and Rylee's stomach growled. She hadn't realized how hungry she was.

The hostess seated them at a table for two with a red and white checkered tablecloth near the front window.

The waitress came over and took their drink order and Hunter immediately handed her both menus. "We'll have a medium deep dish. The house special."

"You got it." The lady jotted their order down on her pad before scooping up the menus.

"Would you like anything else? A salad or breadsticks?" he asked Rylee.

"Breadsticks sound great. I'm starving."

"We'll start with the breadsticks," he told the waitress before she scurried off.

She heard her phone buzz in her purse again. That was the second time since they'd sat down. She fished it out in case it had to do with Liam. She looked down and noticed two missed texts from Avery. *Call me,* was all the last one read.

"Everything okay?"

"Uh, yeah. It's just Avery."

"Do you need to call her? Go ahead."

The room was noisy, but she decided to dial her back anyway. She had a feeling she knew what this was about, but she wanted to make sure.

Avery answered on the first ring, not offering her enough time to prepare for the inevitable conversation. "Rylee, I just heard the news! You and Hunter? Why didn't you tell me?"

"Oh, uh, thank you. It just happened last night. I was going to call you later today."

"Since when do you get engaged and not tell your best friend right away? And how did that even happen? Didn't you just start working for him?"

"Um, yeah, we fell in love quickly. You know, sometimes that just happens. When you know, you know." She didn't know what to say and wasn't prepared to answer questions about her and Hunter. She looked across the table at him and mouthed 'help,' but he just leaned back in his chair with an amused grin on his face.

"Well, I'm happy for you, but are you sure it's not a little quick?"

"We're sure."

"Well, just do me a favor and don't plan your wedding before mine," Avery said in a playful tone, but Rylee knew her friend enough to know she really meant that statement.

"Of course not. I won't steal any of your wedding thunder, I promise."

"I want to hear everything. How did it happen? What does the ring look like?"

"Uh, Avery, I have to go. We're in Chicago and—"

"Chicago? Who are you and what have you done with my best friend? What on earth are you doing in Chicago on a Tuesday?"

"It's hard to hear you, Ave. I'm in a restaurant. Call you later, okay? Bye." She hung up quickly and shoved her phone back in her purse. That conversation wasn't over, but she wasn't prepared for questions about her and Hunter just yet. She would handle Avery later. For now, she just wanted to enjoy the breadsticks that had just arrived.

"How'd that go?" Hunter smirked.

"Not well. Wait until you get to answer questions about us."

"Trust me, I already have."

His admission piqued Rylee's interest. She had been with him all day and hadn't seen him take any calls. "Really? From who?"

"My father. First thing this morning," he said dryly.

"Well, what did he have to say about it?" She dipped her breadstick into the marinara before taking a hot bite that filled her mouth with steam. They must've come right out of the oven.

"That he wants to meet you."

Rylee's stomach knotted, and not from the hunger. "I have to be honest. I'm not really looking forward to that."

"Why's that?" Hunter stopped mid-chew to await her response.

"I don't know. What if he asks how we met? What if he asks questions I'm not prepared to answer?"

Hunter took a sip of his Coke before continuing. "I'm actually glad you brought this up. We need to get our story straight before we start answering anyone's questions."

"So, what's our story?"

He straightened his back and cleared his throat. "I was thinking we would leave out the fact that I'd hired you to clean for me."

A blast of shame hit her. "You mean leave out the fact that I'm your maid."

"No. Well, yes, I suppose." He shifted in his seat. "I mean, just with my father and the board. We'll just say we met through Avery and Shane, which in a roundabout way, is the truth."

"Because you don't want anyone to think you proposed to your maid. I get it." But did she? Even though she was, in fact, his maid, and they were only pretending, the revelation that he wanted to hide it still stung.

"Hey." He reached over the table and squeezed her hand. A current rippled through her at his touch. Could he sense the emotion she was trying to swallow? She looked down at his hand and he quickly retracted it. "I don't mean anything by it. I just think it makes a more believable story that we met through mutual friends and leave the maid bit out. Don't you think?"

Their conversation smacked her back to reality. She had been having fun with Hunter, so much that she'd almost forgotten about their arrangement. His kindness had seemed genuine, instead of something that was just part of a business deal. But she was foolish for thinking it wasn't all part of the act. She didn't fit into his world, and she never would. She had to do better at keeping her guard up. Until yesterday, she'd been sure she would never be interested in someone like Hunter Knox. But something about that kiss had messed with her mind and her emotions, weakening her resolve. If it was only all for show, why did it feel like something more? She hadn't been able to shake the feeling of his lips on hers all day. Not to mention, she'd practically yearned for another kiss at Willis Tower. Why had she been entertaining those thoughts? She'd need to keep her head on straight if they were going to pull this off.

The waitress arrived with the pizza, and Rylee was glad for the distraction. She was ready to shift this conversation to something lighter. She didn't want Hunter to catch on, so she'd have to hide her hurt and change the subject.

"This isn't a pizza; this is a pie!" She had never seen anything like it. It was thick and the sauce was on top instead of under the cheese. She was hesitant, but the gooey cheese that strung from it as Hunter cut her a slice and placed it on a plate in front of her had her belly rumbling.

"Take a bite of that and tell me it's not the best pizza you've ever eaten."

She cut a piece and forked some into her mouth. An explosion of flavors hit her taste buds, and it was heaven. "Okay, you win. This is the best pizza I've ever had."

He had that same amused grin once again. They both ate one piece and were full, especially after eating so many breadsticks.

Hunter had the rest boxed up, and he asked for the check. He glanced at his watch. "We'd better get you back home so you can pick up Liam."

At the same moment he said those words, her mood dampened. That meant their day of fun in Chicago was coming to an end, and for some reason, that left a heaviness inside her heart that she just couldn't shake.

CHAPTER 12

By Wednesday morning, Rylee had decided she wasn't going to take Liam to daycare for the remainder of the week. He would be leaving for art camp soon, and she wanted to spend every second she could with him before he'd be gone for two weeks.

"Get your swim trunks on." She sat on his bed and whispered into his ear to wake him. "How about a day at the beach?"

"Really? You mean, you don't have to go to work today?" His eyes popped open.

"Nope."

"What about daycare?"

She had to laugh. Liam loved daycare, and he didn't seem to realize he only went there when she had to work. "No daycare today, bud."

Liam jumped out of bed and started digging through his dresser drawers. "Brush your teeth and your hair. I'll go pack us a lunch," she told him as she headed for the kitchen. She picked up her lit-up phone from the counter. She had a missed call from Hunter. What could he possibly want? She was really looking forward to spending some time with her son. She picked up the phone to call him back.

"Good morning," he answered.

"You called?"

"I have some good news. I was able to get you a meeting with the listing agent for the studio space downtown. The meeting is tomorrow at 11 a.m."

"You're kidding?" Rylee filled with excitement. Was this really happening?

"I thought I'd go with you, if you'd like. You know, to introduce you and help with negotiations … if you need me."

She hesitated for a moment. Did he think she couldn't negotiate on her own? But then, real estate was what he did for a living. Maybe he really could get her a better deal. "I would like that."

"Great, then it's a date."

"It's not a date. It's business, remember?"

"I didn't mean anything by it." Hunter cleared his throat before continuing, "I also wanted to let you know we have dinner at my dad's this afternoon."

"Today?" She tried to hide the disappointment in her voice. Couldn't he give her more warning?

"Is today not good for you?"

"It's just that I planned to take Liam to the beach for the day. I don't want to have to rush around. Plus, he's not going to daycare for the rest of the week because I want to spend some time with him before he leaves for camp."

"Dinner isn't until five. Does that give you two enough time to go to the beach and for you to get cleaned up and over to my house?"

"I suppose. But I didn't plan to take him to my parent's tonight. I planned for a full day together."

There was a short pause on the other end of the line. "Then why don't you bring him to dinner?"

"Are you sure that's a good idea?"

"Sure, why not?"

"Okay, if you're sure." She still felt hesitant, but how could she tell Hunter no after he'd lined up the meeting for the studio? She just hated involving Liam in the scheme.

"I have an idea," Hunter's voice pepped up. "What if I spend the day at the beach with you and Liam."

"Uh … I don't know if that's a good idea. I mean, I don't want him getting attached to you or anything."

"It's just one beach day. Besides, it would make it more believable if he's comfortable with me this evening. Spending the day together might help."

Of course. Rylee sighed. It was all just a part of the plan.

"We will be at Arbor Shores Beach if you want to stop by. In front of the public access." With that, she hung up. It would be better if he met them there than if they all went together. A part of her wished he wouldn't show up at all.

Maybe if she got lucky, he wouldn't.

Hunter parked his SUV in the public lot next to Ripples and scanned the busy shoreline for Rylee and Liam. It sure was a nice day, and he couldn't remember the last time he'd skipped the office to spend a day at the beach. The noon sun was already high in the sky, and the July temps were expected to reach the upper eighties. Part of him felt like he should be at work making deals, but the other part of him—the part that was beginning to take over his good sense—just wanted to spend some alone time with Rylee and Liam.

"May I join you two?" he asked, walking up behind their

colorful beach umbrella once he'd spotted Rylee. He'd recognize those curls anywhere.

Liam looked up from digging in the sand with his bare hands. "Momma, what's the rich man doing here?" he turned to ask her in a low voice, but not low enough for Hunter to miss.

"Liam, don't be rude. Say hello to Mr. Knox," she told her son with a look of warning.

"Hello, Mr. Knox." Liam looked down at his feet. Disappointment covered his face, and Hunter was at a loss for how to react. Luckily, he had stopped by Callahan's store in town and picked up some supplies to win the boy over.

"You can call me Hunter, remember?" Hunter kneeled down to Liam's level and started digging through the bag he'd brought with him.

"What's in there?" Liam asked, peering to try to see inside the bag.

"I thought you might like to play some Frisbee with me."

"What's Frisbee?"

How was it possible this boy didn't know what a Frisbee was? Didn't he have any male figures in his life who played with him?

"You mean, you've never played Frisbee? Ah, man, you're missing out." Hunter pulled the big yellow disc out of the bag and held it up. Liam's eyes widened with wonder. It was endearing how something as simple as a Frisbee could excite him. He instantly wanted to give him more, but the rest would have to wait. *One thing at a time.*

"You go stand over there, and I'll throw it to you. See how I'm holding it? Now watch how I flick my wrist when I throw it." He demonstrated how he would throw the frisbee, and Liam ran down the beach so he could catch it. When Liam tried to throw it back, it went to the right instead of straight and nearly took out an elderly couple.

"That was good! But this time, hold it level with the ground when you throw it so the wind gets under it. Don't forget, it's all in the wrist."

He could feel Rylee's eyes on them as he waited for Liam to fetch the Frisbee and try again. This time, it went straight and Hunter was able to catch it.

"Nice job, bud! You did it!" Rylee cheered.

Hunter beamed with pride. It felt good to teach this boy something new. They threw the Frisbee back and forth several more times until Hunter began to get winded from chasing Liam's crooked throws.

"How about we take a little break?" Hunter asked after nearly fifteen minutes of playing.

"Mom! Mom! Did you see? I can throw a Frisbee good!"

"I did! You did a great job, Liam. Now, let's let Hunter have a break, okay?"

"Okay." His head dropped and he started toward the shoreline, back to the sandcastle he'd been trying to build.

"Thank you for that." She looked over and smiled at Hunter as he propped his chair up next to hers and took a seat.

"Ah, that was nothing. He's a quick learner."

Looking over at Rylee, she was in a black one-piece swimsuit that accentuated every curve of her lean body. How had he not noticed that sooner? A warmth traveled through him at the sight of her long, toned legs. He tried not to be so obvious, but he couldn't help but admire her beauty. She really was attractive, and for some reason, he was growing more attracted to her each time he saw her.

"So, what am I in for tonight?" she asked, leaning back in her chair and tilting her face toward the sun.

"Well, my dad just wants to meet you, that's all. It will probably just be him and my stepmom, Valerie."

"Are they going to ask questions about us?"

"They might. We're really going to have to act like we're in love."

She sat up straight. "I'd rather not in front of Liam. I don't want to confuse him."

"Could he think we're dating, at least? I'm sure he's seen you date men before, hasn't he?"

"No." She looked down and began brushing sand off her legs.

"You mean to tell me, you haven't dated anyone?"

She hesitated before continuing. "Not since his father," she finally said.

How was that even possible? How could a woman like Rylee not have been wined and dined or taken on dates over the last seven years? She must really be dedicated to her son, and he admired that about her. It made him think about his own mother. After his parents' messy divorce when he was a teenager, she'd moved to Florida to get far away from the humiliation of Carter and Valerie's affair. Hunter had chosen to stay in the family home with his father and Valerie, who had quickly moved in. Even though he spoke to his mother on holidays and birthdays, they were never quite close after the divorce ripped their family apart. A part of him wondered if she felt betrayed that he had accepted Valerie into their family home so easily. She was the mistress his father had been cheating with, after all. A pang of guilt washed over him, and he made a mental note to call his mother and check in.

Liam came running back up to the pair. "Do you want to play Frisbee some more?" he asked Hunter with wide eyes.

"Why don't we go hunt Petoskey stones for a bit? Here, I brought you your very own pail and shovel." Hunter dug through the bag as Liam waited, all smiles.

"You don't need to buy him so many gifts," Rylee leaned over and whispered in Hunter's ear, making him catch a whiff of her intoxicating scent. How could anyone at the beach smell so good?

"What are Petoskey stones?" Liam asked inquisitively.

"They are magical stones that you can't find anywhere else in the world, but I know how to find them here."

"Wow!" Hunter's eyes lit up as he grabbed the pail and shovel from Hunter.

"You are in for a treat. Follow me." Hunter got up and headed toward the shore with Liam, leaving Rylee and her comment at the chairs. He didn't know any other way than to buy this young boy's affection. It was all Hunter had ever known.

Rylee watched as Hunter and Liam scanned the beach for rocks, stopping occasionally to show each other their finds and drop them into the bucket. She hadn't seen her son so excited and full of energy in a long time. Normally, he just drew and kept to himself, but today he was physically active and she had Hunter to thank for it. Perhaps she should consider dating more so that Liam had the chance to learn from a male figure more often.

It tugged at her heart to watch Liam with Hunter because in just two months Hunter would be out of their lives for good, and that might leave Liam heartbroken if he got too close. Luckily, he was leaving for camp soon so he wouldn't have too many opportunities to get attached.

As she watched them together, Rylee could swear Hunter was enjoying himself as much as Liam was. They ran and laughed and took turns digging up the rocks. If Hunter was putting on a show, she didn't know who for. Maybe he wasn't just another rich guy after all. Maybe there was more to Hunter Knox than he showed on the surface.

"Care to join us?" Hunter wandered over and asked as Liam stayed digging at the shoreline.

"Sure." She rose to her feet, meeting him by his side and heading toward the water.

Liam got up, and ran to his mother. "Mom, I'll show you how to find the magic stones! Watch me," he said, and scurried off excitedly in front of them as they slowly walked the shore.

They spent a good portion of the afternoon walking and talking, taking turns digging in the sand with Liam when he'd stop at a new location.

She was sure this was the best day at the beach Liam had ever had, and she was beginning to think she felt the same way.

CHAPTER 13

*H*unter pulled his SUV into Lakeview Estates, and the guard waved him through the security gate. Lakeview Estates was the most prestigious neighborhood in all of Arbor Shores and the surrounding areas, and the Knox estate, where Hunter had grown up, sat high above it all at the top of the hill. The road snaked around sprawling estates boasting pristinely landscaped yards with mansions set far back from the road. When they finally reached the top, and the large chalet-style home came into view, he heard Liam gasp from the back seat.

"Momma, who lives here?"

"Hunter's parents do. I want you to be on your best behavior in front of Mr. and Mrs. Knox, okay?"

Of course, he would. Why was Rylee always minding his manners, anyway? Hunter had never met a kid with better manners before. It was clear she was doing a fine job raising this young boy, but it was a shame he didn't have a father to help him do all the things boys liked to do.

"Are you ready for this?" He turned the car off and looked at her with a hopeful smile, but she looked unsure of herself. Panic washed over her face, and he wondered if they were going to be able to pull this off.

"Ready as I'll ever be." She didn't return the smile or look him in the eye before opening the car door, and that left him feeling uneasy. He watched as she held Liam's door open so he could get out and then quickly took his hand.

Hunter made his way to the other side of the car and held out his hand to Rylee. She looked down at it and hesitated for a moment before placing her other hand in his. It felt so natural there; the feeling of her soft skin sent chills up his arm. He imagined they looked like an all-American family heading up the walkway, hand in hand.

"Momma, why are you and Hunter holding hands?" Liam asked in his usual too-loud of a whisper.

She stopped and turned to her son and knelt down before him. "Liam, Hunter and I like each other. So, if you see us holding hands, that's why."

"Do you kiss?" he asked, and Hunter let out a chuckle. Rylee shot Hunter a look over Liam's shoulder.

"Sometimes. So, don't be surprised if you see that, either."

Liam's cheeks flushed red and a bashful smile lit up his face. Hunter was surprised; he thought Liam may not accept him as his mother's love interest, but so far, he didn't look like the news had bothered him too much.

Rylee may not be into him for anything more than the money she was getting, but at least the kid liked him. For some reason, that made him feel good about himself. He was starting to realize he liked Liam, too.

The front door of the estate opened and a good looking, middle-aged couple came out and headed toward them.

"You must be Rylee. It's lovely to meet you." The beautiful woman with striking blue eyes and long, silky black hair leaned in for an air kiss next to Rylee's cheek. "I'm Valerie Knox, and this is my husband, Carter."

Carter just nodded and looked her up and down with his hands in his pockets. "How do you do?" he finally asked.

"Very well, thank you," she managed to say. This man was intimidating, and just being in Carter's presence was making her uneasy.

"My, you look awfully familiar. Do I know you from some-where?" Valerie asked Rylee, with what appeared to be a pitched brow, although her forehead didn't move all that much. Too much Botox will do that to a person. Valerie had looked familiar to Rylee at first glance, but she couldn't place where she'd known her from. Now, it had come to her why Valerie had recognized her. Her only hope was that Valerie wouldn't piece it together.

"I'm sorry, I don't think so," Rylee managed to get out despite the panic that was rippling through her system.

"Yes, I'm sure of it, but I just can't put my finger on it." Valerie waved her hand in the air. "Ah, well, that's for another time." Valerie shifted her attention to Liam. "Now, who is this handsome young man?"

"This is my son, Liam." Rylee gave Liam's hand a gentle squeeze to remind him to respond.

"Nice to meet you, ma'am. Do you live in this mansion?" Liam looked up at Valerie with wide eyes. "You must be rich like Hunter, but your house is even bigger than his."

An uncomfortable smile spread across Valerie's face, and Rylee felt mortified. Kids always said what was on their minds, right? Hopefully the Knoxes didn't assume those were her words instead of his.

Valerie finally let out a small laugh before Hunter chimed in. "Let's all go inside, shall we?"

Rylee was grateful Hunter had shifted their attention toward the house, and she followed as the Knoxes headed toward the front door, led her through their massive estate, and onto the back veranda. They were quickly met by a butler who approached with a silver tray adorning glasses of iced tea.

"I'm sorry," Rylee said. "Do you have anything without caffeine for Liam? I don't like him to have anything with caffeine so late in the day."

"Of course we do," Valerie said from her seat across the patio. "Jeffrey, why don't you make him one of your famous chocolate milkshakes? How's that sound, Liam?" she asked the boy, and Rylee wondered if she had any children of her own. Clearly not, or she would've known to ask Rylee's permission before pumping her son with sweets. Frustration built up inside her, but Liam's excitement quickly dispelled those feelings.

"Would you like to come help me make it, young man? I have all the toppings you could ever want inside. You can even put your own whipped cream and cherry on top," the elderly butler asked. Liam jumped up.

"Can I, Momma?"

"I don't see why not." She watched as her son followed the butler inside and wondered what that must be like to have a butler on staff. Seemed a little pretentious, but she tried not to judge.

"So, Rylee," Valerie swiveled in her chair to face her. "Beautiful day, isn't it?"

"It sure is." She paused to take a sip of her iced tea. "We spent it at the beach today." She glanced over at Hunter who was leaned back in his chair. This obviously wasn't as uncomfortable for him as it was for her.

"So, that's why you weren't in the office." Carter shot his son a disapproving look, and Hunter sat up straight.

"I worked from home until noon," Hunter told him.

"And what about you, young lady. What is it that you do?"

Carter turned his attention to Rylee, and she could feel the heaviness of everyone's eyes on her.

Here we go. Rylee hadn't prepared for questions like this. She had prepared for questions about her and Hunter, but why didn't it occur to her to prepare for questions about herself? "I only recently relocated back to Arbor Shores from New York City. I'm planning to open a dance studio in town."

"That's wonderful, dear. What kind of dance?" Valerie asked, pursing her perfectly painted red lips around her straw to take a sip of tea.

"Ballet."

Rylee glanced at Carter and noticed he had a suspicious look on his face. "Opening a business in Arbor Shores. That's a big endeavor. Most small businesses fail in the first year. Are you aware of the risks involved?"

Rylee nearly choked on her tea. The nerve of Carter. She'd only just met him, and already he was as tenacious as the reputation preceding him. She opened her mouth to speak before Hunter chimed in and saved her.

"I've informed her of the risks, and we've evaluated the market. There isn't a dance studio within a twenty-mile radius of Arbor Shores. It's a good option."

Rylee was surprised at his response. How did Hunter know that? Had he evaluated the market for her and didn't tell her? He must've been looking out for her, and as much as she didn't need him overseeing her business idea, she appreciated that he'd cared enough to do the research.

"Are you investing in this dance studio?" Carter asked, a pointed look at his son.

"No, she's doing this all on her own. It's her dream. I'll help her negotiate if needed, but that's it." Hunter met Rylee eye's with assurance. She was relieved he'd come to her rescue. She'd be even more relieved when the interrogation was over.

"Wait a minute. It just came to me where I've met you," Valerie cut in, and Rylee's stomach did a flip. "You're the waitress from Ripples, aren't you? My ladies group meets there for brunch the first Sunday of each month. You've waited on us a time or two."

Rylee looked quickly to Hunter. He looked uncomfortable as he straightened his back and shifted in his seat. Valerie had figured it out, and there was no denying how they knew each other now. She didn't feel it was anything to have to hide, but the look on Hunter's face made her think otherwise.

"Yes, that's right. I thought you might look familiar as well but I couldn't place from where." Rylee fibbed. She'd recognized Valerie all right. The demanding customers were always hardest to forget, and she hadn't forgotten how terribly Valerie and her group always treated the staff.

"We usually do brunch at the yacht club, but we try to switch it up now and then. And you can't beat that Bloody Mary bar at Ripples." Valerie winked at Rylee.

"It's one of a kind," Rylee agreed with a forced smile.

"So, you're a waitress," Carter said matter-of-factly. "Opening a business takes quite a bit of money, you know."

How dare he assume she couldn't afford it because she was a waitress. He knew nothing about her. Seething inside, she wished she could tell this man off. But the truth was, he was right, and that's what hurt.

Once again, Hunter came to her rescue before she got any words out. "She has the money for start-up."

Carter rose to his feet. "I'd like to go over the proposal for the Traverse Bay Casino project," he said to Hunter. "In my office."

"Now?" Hunter asked.

"Now."

"You'll be okay for just a bit? I won't be long." Hunter placed his hand on Rylee's knee and a moment of comfort moved through her. Until she realized she'd be left alone to make small talk with Valerie. What could they possibly have in common?

She just hoped there wouldn't be any more questions.

"What do you think you're doing?" Carter barely let the library door slam shut before he started drilling his son.

"What do you mean?" Hunter was confused at his father's anger. He was used to his father's hair-trigger temper, but he couldn't recall anything which would have prompted this.

"That woman is using you for your money! Can't you see that?" Carter paced behind a large mahogany desk as Hunter took a seat in a wingback chair across from it.

"That's not true. You don't know Rylee."

"I don't need to know her to see what's going on here."

"I'm sorry, Dad. But I'm not following."

"She is a single mother with a son. She is a *waitress*," he whispered that final word as if it was dirty and someone would hear him. "Now all of a sudden she has a ring on her finger and wants to open a business? Don't you think there's something a little fishy there?"

"No, I don't. In fact, she had that dream long before she ever met me." Hunter rose to his feet, ready to go head-to-head with his father for the first time in his life. "And she's not a waitress anymore, anyway. She no longer works at Ripples."

"So, you mean to tell me she quit her job after the two of you got engaged? I rest my case!" His father's voice boomed so loud through the office, he hoped Rylee had not come into the house. He was mortified at the thought of her overhearing this conversation.

"I encouraged her to quit her job and follow her dreams. It was my idea, not hers." His fists balled at his sides; he was struggling to keep his cool. "Valerie quit her job when she married you. I don't see the difference."

"How dare you speak of your stepmother like that in this house," Carter spat at his son.

"I'm not speaking anything but the truth."

"Valerie didn't have a child to support or an ulterior motive."

"And you're saying Rylee does? Dad, you're wrong about her." If he only knew how wrong he was.

"I don't like this girl for you, Hunter. I'm sure she's a nice person, but not for you."

Hunter pushed his fingers through his hair and began pacing himself. His temper was at an all-time high, but he had to get it under control. He couldn't blow this opportunity to acquire Knox Enterprises, not after he'd devoted so much of his life to the company, but a part of him also just wanted his father to accept Rylee for who she was. He had a sudden desire to protect her from his father's judgement. Not to mention, he was a grown man, and he was getting tired of his father making all of his important life decisions for him. This was the first serious relationship he'd ever presented to his father, even if it was fake. You'd think Carter would be happy for him. Happy that he'd finally found love.

"She is my fiancée, so I'd appreciate it if you'd give her a chance."

"This is just the type of thing I was worried about. You are not making sound decisions." Carter stormed toward the library doors. "This further makes me believe that you're not ready to take over the company."

"What are you saying?" Hunter asked.

"Figure it out," he threatened, before walking out.

CHAPTER 14

*D*inner was awkwardly silent, besides some random small talk forced by Valerie, which made Rylee wonder what had happened between Carter and Hunter after they'd excused themselves from the veranda. Now they were in the car headed back to Hunter's house, and that same awkward silence filled the air between them.

"Did something happen between you and your father?" Rylee finally asked.

Hunter's eyes stayed fixated on the road. "No, everything is fine."

"Dinner was a bit uncomfortable," she pressed on. "Are you sure it wasn't me?"

"It's just a big business deal we are working on. It has us both under pressure." He finally looked over at her and held her gaze. "It's not you." His words were reassuring, but his voice wasn't. Something was different. Something had shifted since he'd gone inside to speak to his father and it had her feeling uneasy, but she decided not to press the issue any further.

They rode the rest of the way in silence. When they arrived at Hunter's, she woke Liam and told him to get in the backseat of their car so they could go home. Hunter waited for him to get buckled in and walked over to his side of the car to say goodbye.

"Good night, Liam. I had fun with you today," he told him as he started to shut the door.

"Hunter, can I ask you somethin'?"

"Sure, buddy. What is it?" Hunter kneeled in front of the open car door to meet Liam eye to eye.

Liam's sleepy eyes lit up. "When you and my mom get married, can we get a puppy?" The question must've caught Hunter off guard as much as it did Rylee, because he whipped around quickly and glanced at her for help.

Rylee stepped forward and Hunter rose to his feet, backing away to allow her to take over this conversation. "What makes you think we're getting married, bud?"

"I heard you talking to the Knoxes. Plus, you have that ring on." He pointed to her left hand. She had to hand it to her son, nothing slipped past this kid. This is exactly what she was trying to avoid. It was one thing to lie to the Knoxes, but she didn't want to get Liam's hopes up.

"I'll tell you what. We haven't decided any of those things yet, but if and when we decide to get married, you will be the first to know. Right now, we're still trying to get to know each other." At least that part was true, and that's the best truth she could come up with so quickly. "Now, hang on a moment while I say bye to Hunter." She closed the door and met Hunter in front of the car, out of Liam's earshot.

"I wasn't expecting that," he said, a look of shock still spread across his face. "We shouldn't have involved him."

"I'll have a talk with him tomorrow. He'll be fine," she reassured him, but Hunter didn't have that warmth in his eyes that he usually had when he looked at her. In fact, he wouldn't make eye contact with her at all.

He shoved his hands in his pockets and stared at the ground.

"I should let you go. It's getting late," he said after another beat of awkward silence.

"Yeah, I need to get Liam to bed." She paused. "So, I'll see you tomorrow, then? 11 a.m.?" She had a gut feeling he wasn't going to meet her at the studio, but she couldn't bring herself to leave without asking anyway.

"Yeah," he said, almost too quiet to comprehend. "Good night." He turned toward the house and headed for the door.

She sat in her car and watched him disappear into the house, wondering what she'd done wrong, or why he wouldn't look at her. Finally, she turned the key and headed home with an emptiness aching in her chest.

Hunter awoke more conflicted than ever. He threw on a pair of gym shorts and a T-shirt and laced up his running shoes. When he felt like this, a long run along the shoreline usually helped clear his head.

He walked out onto the back deck of his house, greeted by the morning sun and started down the shore. His feet pounded on the sand, the water beside him was eerily calm—a vast contrast from the hurricane of emotions stirring inside him.

So much weighed on him. Should he break off his fake engagement with Rylee? If he did, the board may not deem him a good fit for taking over the business. If he didn't, his father would make sure the business was not left to him. Either way, it was a lose-lose situation. There had to be a way to make both his father happy and impress the board, but how? Perhaps if he could just show his father how great she was, he'd have a change of heart. Perhaps he could change his father's mind at the gala.

But was that even what he still wanted? Last night, the way Liam's face had lit up when he thought they were really engaged was like a knife to his chest. What had he been thinking to involve the boy? He should've known better. The kid didn't have a father figure in his life, and soon, he wouldn't have Hunter, either. It would be better to end this fake engagement now, before either of them got any more attached. If not for his father, at least for Liam's sake. He'd been acting foolishly for wanting to spend time with both of them.

He had a decision to make, but it would have to wait until after the gala Saturday night. Once they got through that evening, they could decide—together—what to do. Right now, he was only sure of one thing. He didn't want to see Rylee and Liam any more than he had to until he could figure this out. Fake relationship aside, he really was beginning to like her, and that was only complicating things more. He had to get her out of his head. Right now, that meant getting in the shower and getting to the office.

That meant not meeting her at the studio.

Rylee checked her watch one more time. Six minutes to eleven. Where was Hunter? She had texted him, but it went unanswered. She tried to call, but it went to voicemail. Whatever had happened last night, something had changed in him. She wasn't sure what Carter had said behind closed doors, but she was sure it had to have been about her.

She would have to talk to Hunter and see what was going on, *without* Liam around. Right now, she wanted him there to help her negotiate this deal. She wasn't even sure what a commercial lease looked like, much less what it should entail.

She glanced at her watch again. Four minutes to eleven.

When she realized he wasn't coming, she called the next best person.

"How's my long-lost bestie today?" Avery answered on the first ring.

"Ave, are you busy?"

"A little, but nothing that can't wait. What's up?"

"Can you meet me downtown right now?"

"For what?"

"I'm here to look at this studio space on Main, and I want to make sure I get a good deal, that's all. You have more experience in business than I do."

"Aw, you mean you actually need me for something?" Avery teased. Rylee knew her friend was probably feeling neglected. She'd been so busy with Hunter that she hadn't seen much of her friends lately.

"Yes, I need you. Can you get here quickly?"

"I'm already walking that way. I was at NovelTea grabbing my morning coffee and scone from Emma. I should be there in thirty seconds."

"Thank you! I owe you one."

"No problem, but why isn't your fiancé with you? Hunter knows more about real estate deals than anyone."

"Long story," she said and hoped her friend didn't pick up on the unsettledness in her voice.

The studio space was every bit as perfect inside as she had envisioned from the outside. Henry, the owner, had showed up with the listing agent eager to make a deal, but Rylee needed to act fast. Commercial space in Arbor Shores never lasted long, and this was the only available space in town. If she wanted it, she would have to sign the lease, pay first, last, and security today since he had interest from another tenant who had viewed it yesterday. That wouldn't leave enough funds for the much-needed renovations to the inside, but she would have her final payment from Hunter in just a few weeks, and then she could rip up the carpet and add hardwood flooring, and have a wall of mirrors and a barre added. She'd also need signage and some advertising to get the word out. She would need to get all of that going right away so that she could open the doors and start bringing in income. Without hesitation, she signed the lease after Avery read it over and gave her the okay. She'd made the right decision. The only thing left plaguing her was why Hunter had stood her up.

"Let's go tell Emma the good news that I'm now her new neighbor." NovelTea was down a side street off Main, which was only a block away from Rylee's new dance studio.

"I would, but I should probably get to the resort. We have deliveries coming in today," Avery told her as they walked outside. "Ry, I'm so proud of you. But I have to ask, where did you get that kind of money?" Avery stood in the parking lot with her hand on her hip, a concerned look on her face.

"What?" Rylee hadn't anticipated that question.

"The money for first, last, and security. That was a hefty check you just wrote."

How could she keep lying to her friend? She was dying to tell her the truth, but if she did, it could ruin everything, and she had given Hunter her word.

"I got a loan."

"From Hunter?"

Avery was being awfully nosy, and Rylee didn't appreciate the interrogation. The high she was riding from signing her lease was quickly diminishing. "Why do you ask?"

"You just seem so ... different lately. First, you quit your jobs. Now, you've taken money from Hunter. It's just not like you. You've always been so independent."

"Hunter is my fiancé, remember?" She recognized that the

words sounded so wrong coming out of her mouth, even as she said them.

"Exactly. And the engagement happened so fast. I just worry for you. If it doesn't work out, what will happen to your studio?"

"It was a loan. He didn't give me the money." It was a white lie, but the way she saw it, she didn't have any other choice. "And what makes you think it's not going to work out between us, anyway?"

Rylee was getting upset now, but she didn't have any right to be. Avery was just trying to be a good friend. Truth was, deep down, the person she was really upset with was Hunter.

$\mathscr{F}$riday morning came, and Rylee still hadn't heard from Hunter. Her anger had now turned to hurt, but she had bigger things on her mind today, like getting Liam checked into camp.

"Ms. Benton, we're so pleased to have Liam joining us," the director greeted them at the reception desk and gave them a property map. "This is Liam's cabin." She drew a circle on the map. "He's sharing with three other boys who I'm sure will be excited to meet him."

Liam moved behind Rylee's legs and latched onto her hand. She thought he'd be more excited when she'd surprised him with the news about camp, but he hadn't wanted to come. He just needed to get used to it, and then surely he'd be fine; he was probably just being shy. She hoped so anyway. The thought of leaving him there twisted at her heart.

"If you want, I can take him and introduce him to the other children."

She knelt down to face her son. "Would you like that Liam? Or do you want me to go back with you?"

"No, Mama. The other boys will tease me if you take me

back." Since he'd been bullied at his previous school, being teased was always one thing that worried him.

"Okay." She wrapped her arms around him tightly for a long hug. "You're going to get to do so much art here, and you'll make friends before you know it. I promise."

She stood up and watched tears well up in his eyes as he looked up at her. It was clear he wanted to go home with her, but he'd never say the words. One thing she admired about him was that he had her strength. Her heart broke into a million pieces, but she had to turn and walk away before he saw the sadness in her own face. It killed her to leave him there, but he'd be happy once he got settled in.

"May I call and get an update from you later?" she asked the director.

"Of course. Call anytime," the kind lady reassured her.

She turned around one last time to watch him walk hand in hand with the director as she carried his duffel bag. They looked deep in conversation, and luckily, he never turned around to see the tears flowing down her face. It was the first time she'd ever left him anywhere for an extended period of time, but why was she so sad? This was good for him and a great opportunity to hone his talent.

Perhaps it wasn't just leaving Liam that had her so upset. These were tears that had been welling up inside her since they'd left the Knox estate last night. And now, she just wanted to go home to her empty house and let them flow.

Hunter sat in his oversized leather chair in his office and twirled a pen between his fingers as he stared out the massive floor-to-ceiling window.

He needed to call Rylee and remind her about the company's

gala tomorrow night. He hadn't spoken to her since they'd left his father's house, and he was feeling a massive wave of guilt for not showing up to the appointment for her studio space. He owed her an apology.

He picked up the phone with hesitation, but finally dialed her number. It rang several times before going to voicemail. Should he leave a message? Nah, a text would do the trick.

Hey, sorry I couldn't meet you yesterday. I got tied up. Just a reminder about the gala tomorrow night. Be at my place by 6 p.m.

He waited several minutes after he sent the text but received no response. He was starting to worry something was wrong. Should he stop by her house and check on her? He couldn't, because he didn't even know where she lived.

At this point, all he could do was wait to see if she'd show up.

Saturday morning, Rylee awoke with an ache in her temples from crying herself to sleep the night before. She had come home from dropping off Liam, put on her pajamas, and ate a pint of ice cream as she binged Hallmark movies, which didn't help with her loneliness. She missed Liam, but why did she also miss Hunter? Was she starting to develop feelings for him? A part of her felt betrayed by his sudden coldness toward her, and then not showing up to the meeting where he'd promised to help her. Another part of her couldn't forget how good he'd been to Liam, and how much fun they'd all had at the beach. She was foolish to think he had actually wanted to spend time with them. Knowing Hunter, he was probably just hoping someone would see them together to make this scheme of his more believable.

She showered and dressed for the day. She had made an appointment in town to have her hair and makeup done for the gala, and she needed to be at the salon at noon. She wanted to look the part for this event; it was an important night for Hunter, and the fate of his future relied on the impression she made on the board. The pressure was enough to make her want to vomit.

She grabbed her phone from the charger on the nightstand next to her bed. She still hadn't responded to Hunter's text from yesterday. It would serve him right to squirm a bit over whether she would show up or not. Now he'd know just how she'd felt waiting at the studio for him. She shoved it into her purse and headed into town, which was just a short walk from the small two-bedroom house she rented.

She loved walking through downtown Arbor Shores, especially on the weekends. The streets were already filled with tourists from downstate who flocked north on the weekends to the popular lakeside town. The sweet scent of honeysuckle growing in her neighbors' yards filled the summer air and mixed with the freshwater smell that the breeze carried off Lake Michigan. She had about fifteen minutes until her appointment, so she decided to stop by her studio.

She had forgotten the key to the studio at home, so she admired it through the large front window. She could already envision what it would be like to have kids lined up, taking ballet classes from her. Excitement bubbled up inside her and washed away any sadness she'd been feeling. Her dream had finally come true, and now she was only weeks away from starting renovations and then opening the doors. She made a mental note to start planning the grand opening party in the meantime.

From there, she headed up Main Street toward the salon, but something caught her eye along the way. There in the window of the Antiques Emporium, sat an old vintage typewriter. She immediately thought of Hunter. It was perfect for him. Even if she was upset with his behavior these past few days, she couldn't help but remember his story about how he'd always wanted one, but his father hadn't supported his dream. He was kind enough to buy all those gifts for Liam, the least she could do was go inside and inquire about the price. Especially since she had ten minutes to spare until her appointment.

"That one in the window? She's a beauty, eh?" The old man behind the counter told her as he pushed his glasses up his nose so he could get a better look at her. "That there is a 1938 Underwood Champion. You don't see many of those anymore. Pristine condition, too. Still has that gloss after all these years."

She leaned in and eyeballed the price tag. It was steep, but she had made up her mind that she was buying it the second she saw it, and there was no spare time for bartering on the price. "I'll take it," she told him before she'd considered what to do with it while at the salon. "Do you ship? It's a gift."

"We can. Gonna be expensive, though. That right there is one heavy piece of machine."

"That's not a problem."

"Here then, fill out this shipping label." He handed her a slip. "Do you want to include a gift card inside the box?"

She considered his offer for a moment. "Yes, please."

He handed her another slip and a pen. She stared at it for a moment and considered what to write before the perfect inscription came to her. She wrote just three words, and handed the slip back to the man along with the shipping label. She pulled out her debit card and handed it over.

The man reviewed the shipping label and chuckled. "Right here in Arbor Shores? Why, that should arrive on Tuesday, then."

She waited for him to run her credit card, signed the slip, and thanked him before heading to the salon, which sat at the corner of Main and Mulberry. Inside, Paula Newman, the busybody middle-aged salon owner, was waiting for her—and not just to do her hair.

"Girl, I'm so glad you're here. We are all ready for the scoop!" She didn't waste any time getting to her point as she sat Rylee in a chair. The two other stylists on either side of her wore smirks on their faces.

"The scoop on what?" Rylee had an idea but hadn't prepared herself for what would come next.

"You and Hunter Knox. The whole town is talking about it."

She took in a deep breath. A moment like this was inevitable, and now that time had come. "Oh, yeah, well, what can I say? It just happened." What could she say? She didn't realize she'd be interrogated this morning, but she should've expected it. This being the only salon in town, it was known for being gossip central in Arbor Shores. She'd have to choose her words carefully so that they wouldn't get twisted.

"Well, from what I hear, you didn't waste any time after you landed that man to quit your jobs."

"Uh, I didn't *land* him, Paula," she corrected her, growing more agitated by the moment.

"Oh, dear, I'm sorry. I shouldn't have said it like that. I mean, nobody can blame you. I know if I were engaged to a man with all that money, I wouldn't work either." She erupted in laughter at her own comment, and the two women beside her followed suit.

"Well, I didn't quit my jobs so that I don't have to work. I am opening a dance studio in town. Just got the keys yesterday." *Shoot.* Should she have told her this? It wasn't exactly how she wanted to announce the studio opening.

"Girl! You're even smarter than I thought. Good for you. You not only got yourself that man, but you also got him to buy you a business."

"No, Hunter did not buy me the business. I am leasing the space and opening it on my own."

"Um hm," Paula peered at her through the mirror's reflection.

"Pay no mind to me. I shouldn't be prying, anyway. Now, what are we doing with this hair of yours?"

Suddenly, the high Rylee had been riding since she stopped by her studio diminished.

Is this really what everyone in town was talking about?

She couldn't wait to get back home.

CHAPTER 16

*H*unter heard the ring of the doorbell and let out a sigh of relief as he glanced at his Rolex. It was 6 p.m. on the nose, and Rylee was right on time. He needed her tonight, and then they could decide if they should break off their fake engagement early and go their separate ways. This way, the board would meet her and think he was settling down, and he'd please his father by ending things shortly thereafter. Of course, he'd still pay her the full payment, so she should be happy to end this arrangement early, especially for Liam's sake. He'd decided he would bring it up on the way home from the gala tonight.

He opened the door to find her standing on his front step, a vision so beautiful he forgot to breathe. She had on the black ball gown he'd bought her in Chicago. Her hair was twisted up in the back with loose tendrils hanging down, brushing her bare shoulders, and the glossiest lips he'd ever laid eyes on. His eyes lingered on those lips as their kiss from the night at the yacht club flashed in his mind, sending a sensation rippling throughout his entire body. It'd only been a couple of days since he'd last seen her, but somehow, he'd forgotten how much he enjoyed the sight of her. Still, it paled in comparison to how he felt whenever she was near.

"You look stunning," he told her as he held the door open for her.

"Thank you."

She was quiet as she made her way in. He realized he'd acted distant when they'd left his father's home, but he'd just been upset with his father, not her. Now he regretted not accompanying her to the meeting for her dance studio.

"I didn't know if you'd come," he finally managed to say.

"Why wouldn't I? It's part of my contractual obligation." Her tone was cold, but her eyes held more of a look of hurt than anger. At some point tonight he'd have to apologize for the past few days and explain his behavior. But right now, they needed to get going.

"Well, I'm glad you're here." He smiled genuinely. "Actually, we need to head out. The limo is waiting."

Was the limo really necessary? Surely, they could've taken his Range Rover to the gala. It seemed a little unnecessary to have a big stretch limo for only two people. She suspected it was more for show than for her.

The driver let them know they'd arrive at the gala in approximately 30 minutes, and then rolled up the partition window. She studied Hunter as he poured them each a glass of champagne that had been chilling in the ice bucket. He sure looked handsome in a tux. When he'd opened the door of his home to greet her, he'd taken her breath away. She couldn't let him know that though. It was clear to her that Hunter didn't have the same feelings for her, and she needed to remember that this was all just a business deal and nothing more.

"To your new studio." He held up his glass after handing one to her.

"How did you know?" She was confused. She hadn't talked to him about the studio. She hadn't spoken to him period since he'd bailed on the meeting.

"I spoke with the agent. He filled me in."

"I was disappointed you didn't show up for the meeting. I tried to call you." No sense in dancing around it.

"I'm sorry about that. I got pretty busy at work with the casino project."

"You should've told me you couldn't come."

"You're right. I should have." He shifted in his seat and adjusted his tuxedo jacket. "I spoke with the agent and reviewed the terms before the meeting since I couldn't be there."

She was shocked by that admission. He'd been looking out for her after all. But still, she'd wanted him there. "Well, that was kind of you, but if you went through all of that trouble it just seems you could've at least sent me a text to tell me you weren't coming."

"I owe you an apology." He leaned over and grabbed her hand and held it softly. "Forgive me?"

His hand was warm and comforting, but why was he holding her hand when there was nobody to see it? Nobody there to put on a show for? "Where is the gala?" she changed the subject.

"Out on the peninsula at the Grand Chateau." Rylee knew of the place, but she'd never been inside. It looked like a castle settled high atop a hill in the heart of the wine region of north-western Michigan. On a clear day, you could see it from miles away.

"Anything I should know going in?"

Hunter dropped her hand and sat up straight. "It's pretty important that the board members meet you and see that I'm happy and ready to settle down, so I'll be introducing you to quite a few people."

"Anything else? Like, what should I talk about? How should I act? Those types of things." She was more nervous going into this event than she'd anticipated. She didn't have much in common with Hunter's crowd of people, and the thought of answering questions about them was a little suffocating.

He placed his hand on her knee, sending a warmth up through her body. "Just be yourself, Rylee, and you'll be absolutely perfect." He turned to look at her with the warmest of smiles, and she thought for a moment he might even kiss her.

She could feel her cheeks flush with color, and if she wasn't mistaken, his were flushed, too. Was he making a pass at her? Or was he just being kind?

He quickly moved his hand off her leg and back onto his, but she could feel the warmth of his touch lingering there, and she didn't want the feeling to leave her.

They drove the rest of the way in silence as they both sipped their champagne and stared out the window.

Walking into the Grand Chateau with Rylee on his arm made Hunter feel like a prince. There was no denying they were a great-looking couple, and this was confirmed as they turned every head in the room when they made their entrance.

Hunter picked each of the board members out from the crowd, and made his rounds introducing Rylee as his fiancée. His plan was working out perfectly, and she seemed to charm everyone they encountered. He was impressed how quick she was to answer questions on the fly, like when they were getting married, how they got engaged, and if they planned to have children right away or wait.

He could feel his father's eyes on them most of the evening, watching their every move. He didn't understand how his father could possibly disapprove of Rylee so much, but he wished he'd give her another chance. Couldn't he see how happy he was with Rylee by his side? Something about her calmed him and brought out a playfulness in him he wasn't used to.

The other set of eyes that followed them the entire night were Marcus Bradley's, and now he was heading in their direction.

"Good evening, Hunter," he said dryly as he approached the couple after dinner. He ordered a scotch on the rocks from the bar behind them and then turned to Rylee. "And you are?"

"Rylee Benton. And you?" she asked, holding out her hand for him to shake.

"Marcus Bradley. I'm the one giving your fiancé a run for his money. Surely, you've heard of me." He took her hand and planted a kiss on the back of it. Heat rose throughout Hunter's body. His jaw began to pulsate.

"No, sorry, can't say that I have." She took a sip of her wine and pulled her hand away from Marcus, looping it through Hunter's arm.

"Well, this engagement seemed to happen rather quickly, didn't it? Tell me, how did the two of you meet, anyway?"

Hunter opened his mouth to speak but Rylee chimed in before he could get the words out. "Through mutual friends. His brother is engaged to my best friend. Plus, we've known each other for years. We went to school together." Known *of* each other would be more like it, but it was only a mild stretch of the truth.

"That's cute, but it seems interesting that nobody had heard of Hunter even so much as dating anyone until Carter announced his retirement."

"Well, I don't know about you, but when I'm dating someone, I like to keep it to myself until it gets serious."

"If you ask me, it all seems rather convenient, if you know what I mean."

"Marcus, I don't know what you're insinuating—" Hunter took a step forward and squared his shoulders. Rylee quickly stepped in.

"Hunter, my love, let's go get some air. It was nice to meet you, Marcus," Rylee said before guiding Hunter in the direction of the veranda.

Hunter shot Marcus a look before allowing Rylee to pull him away. She knew just how to handle the situation, and he found that incredibly attractive. There was even more to this woman than he'd realized.

Out on the veranda, Rylee kept her arm looped through Hunter's as she led him to the side of the building, away from the others who had come outside to enjoy the cool night air. When they reached the other side of the Grand Chateau, they were alone on their own stretch of patio, with nothing but a billion stars above them and acres of grape vines stretched out before them.

It was quiet, the faint sound of music drifting through the air from inside, and the melody of crickets adding their own peaceful hum.

"That guy is a jerk. Don't let him get to you." Rylee turned to face Hunter once they'd reached the railing.

"You handled him like a champ." Was that admiration she detected in his eyes? He was looking at her in a way he never had before. There was a vulnerability about him now that she wasn't used to.

"Well, I spent the past several years in the city, remember? One thing I learned there is how to handle men like Marcus."

"Rylee, I can't thank you enough for tonight." He picked up

her hands and held them, their bodies only inches away from each other. "The way you worked the room and impressed each of the board members. You were a hit. I couldn't have asked for a better fiancée."

"A better *fake* fiancée," she leaned forward and whispered in his ear.

"A *beautiful* fake fiancée," he corrected her. He moved a hand to the side of her face and brushed his thumb softly against her cheek. She took a step back to look at him, but as she did, he stepped forward, closing the space between them, and placed his other arm around her body, gently pulling her into him until their bodies were touching, and she was wrapped in his embrace.

"What are you doing?" she asked in a soft whisper. Whatever it was, she didn't want him to stop.

He moved his mouth close to her ear. "Do you want me to stop?" he whispered, his warm breath on her neck sent chills throughout her entire body.

Her knees began to weaken as he planted soft kisses on the side of her face, slowly making his way toward her mouth.

"No, I don't." Her breath was shallow as she anticipated what was coming next. She allowed her eyes to close at just the moment his warm mouth met hers. He tightened his embrace as she settled into the kiss, placing her arms on his shoulders and running her fingers through the hair at the nape of his neck, pulling him in deeper.

Time stood still; she never wanted the kiss to end. She hadn't been kissed in years, other than their kiss for show at the yacht club. No kiss had ever felt like this. It was as if his lips were made for hers. And since no one was around, the kiss couldn't just be for show.

"Ahem," a man cleared his throat in the distance, and the couple pulled apart. Carter Knox stood with his arms folded by the edge of the building.

"I thought I saw you come this way. Don't you think you two should be getting back to the party?"

"We were just heading back." Hunter smoothed the front of his jacket. Rylee was surprised that a man as confident and strong as Hunter seemed to let his father control his every move.

Carter shot them a disapproving look and turned on his heel to return to the gala.

"We'd better get back inside," Hunter looked to the ground and shoved his hands into his pockets.

They walked in silence, side by side. No holding hands, no arms linked. That coldness about him that she'd witnessed at the Knox estate the other night had returned. Why did his father's presence bring out the worst in him? And what happened to that guy who had just kissed her so passionately out on the patio? It had felt so real. So genuine.

It seemed there were two sides to Hunter Knox, and she didn't care for this side of him one bit.

CHAPTER 17

*H*unter awoke with anxiety knowing Rylee was in his guest bedroom and also knowing what he had to do. He had talked her into staying over instead of driving home after the gala since she'd had a couple of glasses of wine, but now that it was morning, he was wishing he had let the limo driver take her home so he didn't have to have this conversation in person. He'd planned to talk to her the night before, but since they'd both had a few drinks, he didn't feel it was the right time.

But how was he supposed to break off the engagement after that kiss? Now that they'd blurred the lines between fake and real, ending their arrangement seemed like he was actually breaking up with her in a way. If it wasn't for his father's disapproval of her, he would keep this engagement going for as long as she would allow it. He'd grown to like her, and there was something more to that kiss. There was no denying it.

He took a long, hot shower and got dressed before going downstairs to put on a pot of coffee. To his surprise, he found Rylee had already beat him to it. She greeted him with the warmest of smiles as she leaned against the island cupping her mug, wearing a pair of his shorts and one of his T-shirts. He loved the sight of her in his clothes that were too big for her. He took a moment to admire her. He could get used to waking up to her in his home, but that was a thought he had to put out of his mind. It wasn't even an option.

"Good morning," she greeted him with a smile. "I made coffee. I was going to make breakfast but you don't have much in the fridge."

"That's kind of you." He went to move past her and open the cupboard, but her hand moved there at the same time. As their hands brushed, a current shot through him.

"Allow me." She grabbed a mug from the cabinet and poured him a cup. He watched intently as she prepared it exactly how he liked it. How did she know? He turned away and rubbed at the back of his neck. He couldn't look at her. If he did, he'd never be able to do the inevitable.

"I'm glad you're up. We need to talk."

"What is it?" She had a feeling she knew what was coming, and her heart dropped to the floor as she awaited his words.

"I need to end our engagement early." Her heart slammed against her chest. There it was.

"Fine," she said quietly as she put her coffee cup down and began gathering her things from the table.

"Don't you want to know why?" he asked.

"I already know why."

"You do?"

"It's clear your father doesn't approve of me." She wasn't stupid. She'd sensed Carter's disapproval each time she was in his presence. And the way Hunter went from hot to cold whenever his father was around was a clear indication that she was the common denominator.

He took a step toward her, but she headed straight for the door. Her dress was still upstairs, but she'd get it another time. No, she'd just leave it. It's not like she'd ever wear a dress like that again.

"Please don't take it personally, Rylee."

"Why would I?" She turned to look at his face when she reached the front door, and tried with all her might to hold back the tears that were threatening to fall. "It was a business deal, remember?"

"You seem upset. Please come back and talk to me."

"Hunter, I have to go. Liam will be calling soon. No hard feelings. It was only business." *Liam.* The thought of crushing his hopes twisted at her chest. This was really over. What would she tell her son? He was an added layer that made this even more difficult.

"Okay, but I want you to know you'll still get your final payment even though I ended things early. You lived up to your end of our deal, and I appreciate it. Come by tomorrow, and I'll have your final check for you."

She didn't respond, she just turned toward the door and left. It was all she could do to stop the tears from falling, at least until she reached her car.

Once inside, hot tears streamed down her cheeks as she drove up Pine Ridge Way, back toward town. She pulled her car into her driveway and went inside, flopping down on the couch and burying her face in her hands. How could she be so foolish to think that kiss had meant anything? How could she think he would actually consider a real relationship with her?

More importantly, why had she let down her guard and allowed him into her and Liam's lives in the first place?

∽

Rylee didn't know how long she'd been on the couch before she'd drifted off to sleep, but she awoke to the sound of banging on the front door.

"Rylee, let us in."

She peered out the blinds of the front window. It was Avery and Emma. What were they doing there? The last thing she wanted was company but the banging on the door wasn't stopping, so it was clear she'd have to let them in before her headache got any worse.

She shuffled to the front door and opened it to find her two best friends standing there; Emma carrying a box full of donuts and Avery carrying a bottle of wine.

"Wine and donuts?" she asked sarcastically. "What's the occasion?"

"We came as soon as we heard. Are you okay?" They made their way in and headed straight for the kitchen.

"Heard what?" Rylee followed them and watched as they sifted through her cupboards to fish out three wine glasses.

"About you and Hunter breaking off your engagement."

"Wow, good news travels fast, huh?" How could they possibly know? *What* did they know was a better question.

"I'm engaged to his brother, remember? Don't worry, the whole town doesn't know." Avery looked at her sympathetically. "Not yet, anyway," she added.

Emma held out the box of donuts to Rylee, but she didn't have an appetite. She shook her head and then shuffled back to the living room to take a seat on the couch.

"So, what happened?" Emma asked.

Rylee's heart skipped a beat and then plummeted. She didn't have the energy to think up a lie, and to be honest, she didn't feel like lying to her friends any longer.

"Nothing happened. It was all a fake engagement so Hunter could land his father's company." It came out before she could consider her words, but she instantly felt better having the truth out in the open.

"What?" Avery put down her wine glass and sat up straight.

"It's true. It was all one big fake engagement."

"Why didn't you tell me, Ry? You mean, you lied to me? To us?" Avery looked hurt.

"Please don't be upset. I was sworn to secrecy. It was in the contract. I didn't know how to tell you two. I couldn't."

"What about the studio? What will happen there?" Emma asked.

"The studio is mine. I paid for it with the deposit he paid me to go along with his plan."

"I knew he was a dirty rat!" Avery stood up and began pacing the room.

"You mean he paid you? I don't think I'd tell anyone that, Rylee." Emma had a disapproving look on her face.

Rylee looked down at her hands and twisted at the tissue she was holding. She shouldn't have told them. What was she thinking? It just came out.

"It was a business deal, and I'm not telling anyone. Only you two know, so please don't say anything. I had to sign an NDA."

"You mean he made you sign paperwork?" Avery was still shaking her head in disbelief.

"Yes, it was all part of the deal. So, you can't tell anyone, including Shane. Promise?" She looked up at Avery with hopeful eyes.

Avery hesitated. She had a look of anger and hurt on her face, but Rylee knew her friend would calm down. "Okay, but I have to say I'm surprised at you, Ry. This just isn't like you."

"I made a bad decision. Can we please be done with it? I feel bad enough as it is."

"You feel bad that you lied?" Avery wasn't letting this go as easily as she hoped.

"Of course I feel bad about that. But I also feel bad that it ended. I think I was actually falling for him." There, she'd said it. It was the first time she'd admitted her feelings for Hunter. Even to herself.

"Aw, Ry!" The look of hurt and anger instantly disappeared from Avery's face as she rushed to Rylee's side. "Did you tell him how you feel about him?"

"Of course not."

"You have to tell him!" Emma chimed in. "Maybe he feels the same way about you."

"Trust me, he doesn't."

"How do you know unless you tell him?"

"I just know." Rylee could no longer resist the box of donuts in front of her. She reached in and fished out an eclair and took a bite. "Now can we please change the subject? I don't want to talk about this ever again."

Avery and Emma stayed with Rylee until they'd finished the wine, and Rylee did her best to be a gracious hostess, but she was relieved when they finally left. She was tired of putting on a brave face for her friends, and she just wanted to wallow in her pity one last day.

Tomorrow, when she woke up, she'd put Hunter Knox behind her once and for all, and get back to normal life as she knew it.

CHAPTER 18

"*W*hat are you doing here, bro?" Hunter asked as he opened his front door to find Shane standing on his front step.

"Can't I stop by to see my kid brother?" Shane asked, six pack in hand. "Come on, let's sit out back and have a beer. We need to talk."

Hunter didn't feel like company, but he sure could use a beer at a time like this. He'd felt terrible all day since he'd broken things off with Rylee. He hadn't had many real relationships, but he imagined this was what a real break up felt like. It was the closest thing he'd had to one, anyway.

They both took a seat on the back patio just as the evening sun was sinking into the horizon. Shane cracked a beer and handed it to Hunter, then opened one for himself. Hunter took a long hard pull, hoping it would dull the pain festering inside him. No such luck.

"What's going on with you and Rylee?" Shane finally broke the silence.

"Exactly what I told you this morning on the phone. We broke off our engagement."

"I know what you told me on the phone, and I also know there was no real engagement." His brother looked at him pointedly.

Hunter's stomach dropped. "What? What are you talking about?"

"You can stop playing dumb with me. I know all about the fake arrangement and the ploy to get the family business."

Heat shot through Hunter's body. He couldn't believe Rylee had betrayed him. "Who told you?"

"Who do you think?"

"You can't tell a soul, Shane. Promise me." Panic took over, and Hunter rose to his feet.

"Of course not. You know I don't have any interest in the family business, and I surely don't have any interest in talking to Dad. Your secret is safe with me." Shane took a drink from his beer and Hunter sat back down. "But what I really want to know is why you would let a girl like Rylee get away?"

Hunter put down his beer and shoved both hands through his hair, looking toward the sky. "It was just a business deal. And that deal has ended." He tried to sound convincing, but who was he trying to convince? Shane or himself?

"You mean to tell me you don't have any feelings at all for Rylee?"

"It doesn't matter if I did. Dad thinks she's only out for my money, and he doesn't approve of her. Basically, if I'm with Rylee, I lose the business to Marcus Bradley."

Shane laughed.

"What's so funny?" Hunter shot a look at his brother.

"You don't see anything wrong with that?"

"Of course I do, but that's the way it is. I've worked far too hard in this business to lose it all to Marcus. I have no choice but to walk away from Rylee."

"You always have a choice. And sometimes, money isn't everything. Remember that." Shane got up and crushed his empty beer can before setting it on the patio table. "Have you ever considered standing up to Dad?"

"You know as well as I do how that would end."

"I do, and I've lived a pretty good life because of it. Sounds like you have some serious thinking to do." He grabbed the rest of the six pack and tossed it in Hunter's lap. "The rest are for you; you're gonna need them."

Shane showed himself out, and Hunter was left feeling worse than before his brother had gotten there. Shane was only giving him some tough brotherly love, but didn't he understand the position Hunter was in? All Hunter knew right now was that he couldn't wait to get ahold of Rylee. Even if he *had* been falling for her, he couldn't get over this betrayal. He never thought she would tell anyone about their arrangement. He had trusted her. This just showed she wasn't the person he thought she was after all. Perhaps his father was right about her.

The one thing he was certain of was that this ruined everything, including their monetary agreement.

Rylee emerged from her long, hot bubble bath to find she had a missed call from Hunter. Should she call him back? What could he possibly have to say? Their fake relationship was over, so she really didn't have any need to talk to him, unless he was calling to tell her what time to stop by tomorrow to get her final check. She'd better give him a call back to arrange the pick-up. The sooner she got that check, the sooner she could start renovations on the studio and get the doors open.

"Hey, you called?" she asked when she heard him answer.

"You breached our contract," is all he said on the other end.

"What are you talking about?"

"Page two, Section E states that if you told anyone about our agreement, it would be null and void, and you wouldn't get your final payment."

"I know what the contract says." She swallowed hard. Is it possible that Avery had said something? No way; she had promised.

"Then why was my brother just here drilling me about our arrangement? You signed an NDA, remember?"

"I know what I signed, Hunter. I'm sorry. Avery came over today demanding answers, and I didn't have it in me to lie to her any longer."

"Well, that was your choice, but we had a deal."

"So that's why you called?" She was secretly hoping he'd called to say he missed her and that he'd made a mistake.

"Why else would I have called?" His words were icy and they stung.

"Keep the money, Hunter. It's all you seem to care about anyway."

She hung up and tossed the phone on the counter. Then she picked it back up and searched his name in her contacts list and blocked his number. She didn't need Hunter or his money. She'd worked hard for everything she had, and she didn't need him or that final payment to get her studio open.

Tomorrow, she would get busy making her dreams happen on her own.

Hunter was left standing with the phone to his ear but nobody on the other end of the line. Her words slapped him upside the head, and he'd never felt worse about himself in his life as he did today.

First, he'd let Rylee slip away only to please his father. Then, his brother's disappointment in him served as a dose of hard love and sour reality. Finally, he'd taken money from Rylee that she needed for her studio, and all he was left with was more money than he needed, a big empty house and nobody to share it with, and a father who was impossible to please.

What had he done? Had he made the wrong decision by calling Rylee? He'd just been so angry. He'd felt betrayed, and he'd let his anger get the best of him.

He picked up the phone to call her back and apologize but it went unanswered. Should he find out where she lived and go to her house? No, he'd done the right thing. There was no way he could trust her now, even if he wanted to. She had betrayed him, so it would be best just to get her out of his mind once and for all.

CHAPTER 19

*R*ylee pulled her car in front of Arbor Shores Resort and shut off the engine. She didn't realize how much she'd missed this place until she got there. Inside, she made her way through the employee entrance, heading straight for Avery's office. She was pleased to find her friend inside doing paperwork.

"How could you tell Shane?" she asked as she closed the door behind her.

"Hey, Ry. What are you doing here?"

"You promised."

"I was only looking out for you. I could tell you had developed real feelings for Hunter, and I knew Shane would talk to him since you wouldn't." She stood up and made her way around the desk. "Don't worry, I swore him to secrecy."

"It doesn't matter if you swore him to secrecy. He talked to Hunter about it, so now Hunter knows I breached our contract."

"Oh, you're just overreacting."

"I'm not overreacting. Hunter isn't paying me my final payment. Now I have no way of getting the renovations done on the studio, and I'm stuck with a monthly lease I can't afford."

Avery pulled Rylee in for a hug. "I'm so sorry, Ry. I had no idea he would do something like that. Are you sure?"

"I'm positive. He called last night to tell me."

"Wow. Please know I would never have sent Shane over there if I thought it would hurt you. We were only trying to help."

"I know you wouldn't." Rylee collapsed into the chair and tossed her head back. "What am I going to do now?"

"You can have your job back here. Does that help?"

"I was hoping you would say that."

"You'll just have to work hard to make extra money to get the studio open, but you can do it. I know you can. You're one of the hardest working women I know."

"That's all I can do, I suppose."

"Have you talked to Ripples?"

"Yep. I start back there later today."

"See? It will all come together." Avery had compassion in her eyes and Rylee could tell her friend didn't mean any harm. No sense in staying mad at her.

Rylee was just thankful she'd had the good sense not to quit her jobs and instead taken a leave of absence back when Hunter's crazy arrangement was presented to her. At least she had Ripples and the resort to fall back on. Now all she could do was work extra shifts and save every cent for renovations. With any luck, she'd get her studio open by the end of summer.

Hunter had no desire to go to the office Monday morning, and by Tuesday he decided he still wasn't ready to face his father, so he'd work from home the rest of the week.

Around noon, he left his home office to make his way to the kitchen. There had to be something in his fridge to eat. As he stared into the empty fridge blankly, hoping something would magically appear, he heard the doorbell ring. Who could it possibly be? He prayed it wasn't his brother. He couldn't take another visit from Shane or another dose of his tough love. Not this week, anyway. He was trying to keep his head on work, and Shane forced him to think about impossible things. Things that he'd resolved to put out of his mind once and for all.

He opened the door to find the postman had left a box on his porch and was heading out of the driveway. He leaned down to pick it up, and was surprised at how heavy it was. He carried it to the kitchen and placed it on the island, grabbing a knife from the drawer to cut the tape. He opened the lid and couldn't believe his eyes. The most beautiful vintage typewriter he'd ever seen was inside, in pristine condition. He pulled it from the box and placed it on the counter and punched a few keys. He loved the sound they made; it was like music to his ears. It was the best gift he'd ever received. But where did this come from? If it was from his father, he was about fifteen years too late. There was only one other person who knew how much he'd always wanted a typewriter.

He peered inside the box to see if there was anything else inside. Just a small white envelope. He pulled it out and opened the back, pulling a plain white card from inside. A simple inscription told him exactly who the gift was from. Three words told him all he needed to know. The card read:

Follow your dreams.

And nothing else. Just when he thought he couldn't feel any worse, he dropped to his knees right there in his kitchen.

CHAPTER 20

ONE MONTH LATER

*I*t was the end of August and the temperature was at a record high for Arbor Shores. The last thing to get fixed in the studio was the air conditioner, and it got serviced in the nick of time for the grand opening. Rylee had been running around all day gathering last minute supplies for the event, and she'd managed to squeeze in a quick stop at home to shower and change before guests were set to arrive at the studio.

"Do I have to wear this tie, Momma? It's hot," Liam asked as he tugged at his collar.

"Just for a little while. I'll let you take it off in a bit; I promise." Rylee admired her son. He was growing up so fast, and she could swear he'd grown at least an inch while away at art camp this summer. She was just glad he had enjoyed himself and was now home to spend some time with her before the kids went back to school.

She took a final look in the mirror and hoped she looked presentable in her sky blue knee-length dress and nude flats. She had invited members from the Chamber, and she was hoping the studio would be filled with parents and potential students. Her goal was to enroll enough students tonight to start the three class times she'd be offering. That's all she could fit in with her busy work schedule at Ripples and the resort, but at least it was a start.

The ride to the studio was quick since they only lived a few blocks away. Once they arrived, she was pleased to find Emma setting up the baked goods and refreshments that NovelTea had donated, and Avery and Shane were putting balloons and the grand opening sign out by the road.

She took a moment to admire all she had done to get Benton's Ballet Company open in just four weeks. Luckily, Shane had offered to lay the flooring and install the wall of mirrors, which saved her on labor, and she was able to work out a deal with the sign company to make payments on her signage and installation. She'd joined the Chamber of Commerce and attended local mixers to get the word out, and opted for a small ad in the *Arbor Shores Beacon* for the grand opening party. She had worked hard over the past month to pull this off. The fact that she'd done it on her own—*without* Hunter's money—felt really good.

Parents and children began to arrive, and she took the time to speak to each person and show them around the studio. For two solid hours, the studio was filled with locals who'd come out to either support her efforts or inquire about her classes.

By 8 p.m., when the last parent and child left, she had filled all three classes she was offering. With their registration fees paid on the spot, she now had enough to pay her next month's lease payment, which had been weighing on her for a month.

"You did it, Ry! We're so proud of you." Avery said after the last guest left. She stood with her arms around Shane's waist.

"Thank you both for all of your help. You too, Emma," she called to Emma who was breaking down a table in the corner. "I couldn't have done this without all of you."

"I'm sure you could have, but that's what friends are for." Avery gave her a wink.

A knock on the door got all of their attention. It was dark outside now, so she couldn't tell who it was through the window, but she assumed it was a latecomer.

She twisted the lock and opened the door to find Hunter standing there with a bouquet of flowers and a puppy by his side. Rylee's heart palpitated in her chest. She hadn't seen him since the morning after the gala. He looked handsome as ever standing there in his black polo shirt and faded blue jeans. But he was the last person she expected to see, and honestly, she had hoped she'd never have to see him again. What was he doing there, anyway? And why did he bring a dog with him?

"I wanted to come by and congratulate you on your studio opening." He had a hopeful look in his eyes. "Here, these are for you." He handed her the flowers.

She reached out for the flowers and smelled them. "Come in," she said softly, stepping aside so he could enter, along with the chocolate Lab puppy he had on a leash next to him. The puppy was adorable, she just hoped he wouldn't have an accident on her new hardwood floors.

"Hunter!" Liam yelled out from the chair he'd been sitting on while coloring. He got up and ran over, throwing his arms around Hunter's legs and giving him a big hug before dropping to his knees to pet the dog.

"Hey, Liam. Good to see you." Hunter ruffled Liam's blond hair. He looked genuinely excited to see Liam, which softened Rylee's heart just a tad, although her guard was still up with him and she was not thrilled about Liam seeing him. He'd already asked about Hunter several times, and each time he had, it broke her heart a little more.

"Is this your dog?" Liam looked up at Hunter as the puppy leaned in and licked at Liam's face, which made him erupt in giggles. Rylee had never seen him look so happy.

"I just got him, and I've been having the hardest time coming up with a name. I was hoping you could pick out a name for him."

"Really?" Liam beamed. "How about Duke?"

"Duke is perfect." Hunter smiled down at Liam, while the puppy took the opportunity to get another lick of Liam's face.

"Hey, Liam, how about we take the puppy to the park across the street?" Emma chimed in, and Rylee mouthed the words 'thank you' to her friend.

"Okay! Will you be here for a little while, Hunter?"

"Probably not, buddy. I just stopped by to say hello and see the studio. But you can take Duke to the park for a bit."

"Okay. Maybe we can go to the beach again before school starts?"

"I'd like that." Hunter smiled warmly at the boy.

"Come on, Liam." Emma took the leash in one hand and Liam's hand in the other and guided them out the door.

"We need to get going as well," Avery said as she pulled Shane toward the door.

Rylee watched as Shane nodded at Hunter as he passed and gave him a look of approval, as if he was proud of him. It had to be Shane who had told him about the grand opening. She was sure of it.

When the door closed, they were left alone standing in the middle of the studio. Soft music played quietly through the speakers, and she already had dimmed the lights before he arrived as they were getting ready to close up for the evening.

"What are you doing here?" she finally asked.

"I wanted to come by and congratulate you on your studio. I'm really proud of you, Rylee." He took a step closer, but she turned her back and walked over to the corner of the room to put down the flowers. She was finding it hard to face him without breaking down. She'd been so strong over the past month. She'd kept herself so busy with opening the studio that she hadn't had time to think about her heartbreak. Now, just the sight of Hunter had a sea of emotions swirling inside her.

"Thank you, but why are you really here?" She turned around to face him. She wanted him to look her in the eye and tell her why he was there.

"Because I miss you. And I wanted to apologize for the way I acted." He took a few steps toward her and held out his hand. "Dance with me?"

She looked down at his hand and hesitated before giving in and taking it. She'd had a month to cool down, and she was running out of reasons to be upset with him by the minute.

"I'm the one who owes you an apology," she said as he pulled her in for a slow dance. They swayed back and forth in the middle of the studio, and the familiar smell of his cologne reminded her just how much she had missed him. "I'm the one who broke our contract and betrayed your trust. For that, I'm sorry."

"No, I overreacted. I should have given you your final payment, and I want you to still have it."

"No." She was quick to respond. "I don't want it. I can do it on my own, and I have."

"I know you have. What you've done is incredible."

"What about you?" Her body began to soften and she leaned closer. She could feel his warm body pressed up against hers, and it was a comforting feeling she had missed since their kiss at the gala. "Have you taken over Knox Enterprises?"

"It was offered to me, but I turned it down."

"What?" She stopped dancing and took a step back to look at him. "Why would you do that? It was your dream."

"No, it was my father's dream, and it took me some time to realize I was living for him instead of following my own dreams. You've inspired me to follow my passion."

"So, what are you going to do now?"

"I started my own publishing company. And, thanks to you, I've also started writing my novel."

"That's fantastic." She leaned back into him and he wrapped his arms more tightly around her waist this time. She rested her head on his shoulder in a moment of surrender. "How'd your father take it?"

"Better than expected. Turns out, once I stood up to him, he started treating me more like a man of respect. He's decided to postpone his retirement until, and I quote, 'I come to my senses.'"

"And when will that be?" she asked.

"I'm pretty happy with what I'm doing. I'm finally doing something for me, and I no longer have to answer to my father or live to make him happy. That feels good."

"I'm happy for you, Hunter. You deserve it."

"There is one thing missing though." He stepped back to look into her eyes.

"What's that?"

"You." He cupped her face in his hands gently and placed his mouth on hers, kissing her ever so lightly at first, then more passionately as she wrapped her arms around his neck and deepened the kiss. They continued to embrace until the song came to an end, then he planted one final kiss on her forehead before she rested her head on his chest.

"Rylee, I not only fell for you, but I fell in love with Liam, too. I want to be the positive father-figure for him that I always longed for. He deserves it. You both do. You made me realize all the wealth and success in the world doesn't matter if you don't have someone special to share it with. I want to share my life with you and Liam. If you'll have me?"

"We'd like that. So, where do we go from here?" she asked in a dreamy tone.

"No rules this time." He held her tightly and placed his chin on top of her head. "This time, we just love each other and see where that takes us."

"Does that mean you love me?" She looked up at him with soft eyes.

"Of course, I love you," he said without hesitation.

"Good, because I love you, too."

EPILOGUE

*E*mma held Liam's hand outside of the studio window as they stood and watched Rylee and Hunter slow dance under the dimmed studio lights. She and Liam had been at the park with Duke for quite some time, but she didn't want to interrupt the two lovebirds until this last song ended.

Liam beamed with excitement at the sight of his mother and Hunter together, and Emma felt so happy for her friend that she'd finally found someone to give her the love that she and Liam deserved.

Watching the couple dance together made her think about her own love life. She was a hopeless romantic; she owned a bookstore filled with love stories and happily ever afters, but she'd yet to find true love of her own. In fact, she hadn't had a serious relationship in years, always too busy running NovelTea, and when she wasn't at work, she was a bit of a bookworm. That's probably why she'd always gotten lost in romance novels, so she could live vicariously through the love stories of others.

But seeing Rylee and Hunter's story unfold gave her hope that maybe happy endings do come true and are not only reserved for fairy tales and romance novels.

Maybe her Prince Charming was somewhere out there ready for love, too.

Will Emma ever find her real-life Prince Charming? Find out in Book Three: *Conquering the Heart of the Bad Boy.*

ABOUT THE AUTHOR

Nomi Summers is a clean contemporary romance author with a flair for taming bad boy heroes readers swoon over.

When she's not dreaming up her next small town romance, you'll find her at the beach devouring the latest new release on her Kindle. Her other guilty pleasures include getting lost in mindless reality TV and spending far too much time talking to her dogs, as she's convinced they understand every other word!

Nomi's living her own "happily ever after" with her loving husband and their two fur babies in Tampa Bay, Florida. However, a piece of her heart will always belong in Michigan where she's originally from—the inspiration behind the settings in her novels.

www.ingramcontent.com/pod-product-compliance
Lightning Source LLC
Chambersburg PA
CBHW071124100726
47908CB00008B/2483